Praise f  less and

"This is the '80s . . . but the humiliations and pretensions are time-
less . . . McCandless . . . hilariously captures teen politics . . . there's
compassion beneath the dead-on details . . . [a] polished debut."

—Lori Gottlieb, *People* (three stars)

"McCandless skewers 80s adolescence."

—Tina Jordan, *Entertainment Weekly* (Recommended Beach Reading)

"McCandless' story is like those light and breezy girl books we
used to read in middle school, only filtered through the gimlet eye
of adulthood. Norrie's illustrations also add a great retro feel to the
perfect coming-of-age story for a generation raised on Wham! and
Bonnie Bell lip gloss."

—Rebecca Swain Vadnie, *Orlando Sentinel*

"A witty look at what it takes to be accepted . . . [and] the inevitable
pitfalls of growing up."

—Sarah Frame, *The Detroit News*

"Sensitive, compassionate, and tender . . . written with exceptional
clarity and nonjudgmental honesty . . . highly entertaining."

—Alex Suczek, *Grosse Pointe News*

"[A] frank, funny look at teen girl culture and crisis...reminiscent of the honest, straightforward stories once penned by teen-fiction legend Judy Blume ... McCandless manages to make the reader aware of how much people already understand, and willfully ignore, of the world around them in those hateful/halcyon years."

—Kelly Clarke, *Willamette Week Online*

"A hilarious, spot-on survey of the humiliations and perilous victories of a privileged adolescence...McCandless' wickedly funny descriptions and her unerring ear for teen dialogue will appeal to any reader who remembers, or is surviving, the stomach-twisting anxiety of becoming an adult."

—Gillian Engberg, *Booklist*

"Sarah Grace McCandless writes with humor and compassion and honesty about the most embarrassing time in all our lives, those terrible years between the first crush and the first orgasm. No matter which side of the tracks you come from, *Grosse Pointe Girl* will hit you where you live."

—Pam Houston, author of *Cowboys Are My Weakness*

"Sarah Grace McCandless is a flat-out fantastic writer. Among her many gifts is an ability to combine laugh-out-loud humor with an unaffected, devastating sadness. The result is absolute magic—the strange, beautiful truth about childhood revealed."

—Joe Weisberg, author of *10th Grade* (an *Entertainment Weekly* Top Ten Book)

the girl i
wanted to be

A Novel

Sarah Grace McCandless

Simon & Schuster Paperbacks

New York   London   Toronto   Sydney

SIMON & SCHUSTER PAPERBACKS
Rockefeller Center
1230 Avenue of the Americas
New York, NY 10020

First Simon & Schuster trade paperback edition 2006

SIMON & SCHUSTER PAPERBACKS and colophon are registered trademarks of Simon & Schuster, Inc.

Book design by Ellen R. Sasahara

Manufactured in the United States of America

10   9   8   7   6   5   4   3   2   1

Library of Congress Cataloging-in-Publication Data

McCandless, Sarah Grace.
    The girl I wanted to be : a novel / Sarah Grace McCandless. ——
1st Simon & Schuster trade pbk. ed.
        p. cm.
    1. Teenage girls—Michigan—Fiction. 2. Michigan——Fiction. I. Title.

PS3613.C34525G57 2006
813'.6—dc22

ISBN-13   978-0-7432-8518-6
ISBN-10   0-7432-8518-2

For information regarding special discounts for bulk purchases, please contact Simon & Schuster Special Sales at 1-800-456-6798 or business@simonandschuster.com.

To the girls I wanted to be—
Carey, Daphne, Maria, and my mom.

Acknowledgments

First and foremost, I'm extremely grateful and honored to have the opportunity to once again work with Denise Roy, an editorial genius and incredible human being who brings out the best in everyone. Thank you to everyone at Simon & Schuster, especially David Rosenthal, Victoria Meyer, and Annie Orr. Special thanks to Michael Accordino and Christine Norrie for your creative ideas and your patience. And of course, none of this would be possible without my fearless leader Jenny Bent and the Trident Media Group. You da best.

I continue to have deep appreciation and admiration for the writers, artists, and performers who inspire me, including Wes Anderson, Judd Apatow, Melissa Bank, Cameron Crowe, Tina Fey, Lisa Glatt, Peter Hedges, Pam Houston, Chris Martin, Shawn McBride, Lorrie Moore, Sarah Silverman, Joe Weisberg, and Rachel Yamagata. You're all invited to my next birthday party—chardonnay will be served.

I'm very grateful for the support from an amazing network of people I'm privileged to call friends—Scott Allie, Bozzi, Bob Harris, Jimmy Fillmore, Steve Jaquith, Rich Johnson, Jeff Macey, Kim McFarland, Abby Mims, Misty Osko, Jamie S. Rich, Michael Ring, Carla Slomski, and Tim Williams. Also, thank you to my friends in the comics industry, which is indeed like the Mafia—once you're in, you're never really out. Many thanks to my new DC crew for making me feel at home, especially Clay Dunn, Sean "Arnie" Carroll, Jeff Liesch, Paul Roberts, Lisa "Nell" Aragon, Andi Gabrick, and Corrie Zielinski (you're still DC to me). Thanks to Lauren Cook for the title and brainstorming, to my research partners at The Ice Shanty Fishing Forums, and to Jeff Kass and The Neutral Zone for inviting me to be a part of your amazing program.

Big thanks to my family for their unwavering support and to my nieces Anna Grace and Ella Kathryn for making me pee my pants. Thanks also to the DeLaurentis family for treating me like one of their own. Most of all, thank you to Ian Sattler, my partner-in-crime, whom I love more than homemade macaroni and cheese, cupcakes, and Halloween, combined.

And finally, I want to thank every single person who read my first book, and this one, and all of those to come. SGM + you = best friends forever.

the girl i wanted to be

Chapter 1

The Family Reunion

On the last day of our family reunion, we roast a pig in the backyard, which really is the beach and then it turns into the lake. I ask Dad if a tide will come in and drown the pig, and my cousin Barry, who is seventeen and has started to shave, says, "Presley. It's already dead." Then he scoops up a handful of sand and sprinkles it over my head. Even though I know I'm going to have to unbraid my hair, shake the sand loose, maybe even wash it again, I don't say a word, because Barry is bigger and stronger and also the cutest of all the cousins. His dad, my uncle Tim, who is digging a grave for the coals, turns to catch Barry salting me like an ear of corn, and when he shouts out Barry's name— first, middle, and last—Barry dashes into Lake Michigan and swims fast beyond the bobbing red buoys, far away from a spanking he has long outgrown.

At nine o'clock in the morning, it's already 84 degrees. Dad says it will take all day to roast the pig, even with the coals simmering underneath its belly and the sun dissolving in the sky above. I pull on my sandy braid with one hand and, with the other, tug at my purple one-piece that's grown tight since we bought it in June, when summer began and eighth grade finally came to an end. Mom says it's too close to the end of the season to buy a new one, and now I've got this suit that creeps into places it has no business going. I catch Dad raising his eyebrows as I try to sneak my suit back into place, so I grab my jean shorts from the patio chair and hoist them over my hips to hide what happened these past few months, this expansion I cannot seem to control.

"Better shake that sand out of your hair before your grandma sees it on her clean floor," Dad says.

"I'm not going inside. I'm going out front to roller-skate for a while."

"Well, don't go too far." He calls Uncle Tim to help him lift the pig up over the fire. The pig is stretched out and bound to a stick and looks like it fell asleep during a magic trick. Last year I had to do a group project on farm animals, and Misty Thompson, who wore only designer jeans paired with various cotton-candy-pink angora sweaters, quickly took charge of the assignments. I got stuck with the pig, and other than it being a main dish, the only thing I could remember was how farmers would sometimes train them to find little tumors of fungus buried in the ground below. That and their tendency to pee in their own trough. I cannot imagine eating any pig. I don't want to see my meat in its natural state, in the shape and form it took as a living thing. I prefer a flat, boneless chicken breast cloaked under cream-of-something sauce.

I'm slowly backing up toward the porch where I left my skates when Betsi, my mom's sister, pops her head over my shoulder and whispers, "Not a chance in hell I'm eating any of that," and then she makes loud snorting sounds. I giggle and plop down on the patch of lawn to pull on my royal-blue skates blackened with skid marks. Betsi crouches down to help me with the laces.

Betsi was only a teenager when I was born, and because she still understands why I roll my eyes when Mom tells me to wear a hat and scarf in the winter, I've never called her Aunt anything, just Betsi. She ties my laces extra tight, and when I stand up on my skates, ready for motion, I spot my brother, Peter, through the back windows of our cottage. He's sitting in the big beige recliner, the upholstery worn soft like the fur of an old dog. Barry would kick Peter out, but he's still seeking refuge in the water, so Peter basks on his temporary throne. He's nursing a bowl of soggy cornflakes, milk dripping from his spoon onto the book about earthquakes balanced on his knees. Peter's only nine, but he never had to learn how to read, he just knew. On road trips to Florida to see the grandparents, Dad would ask me to read billboard signs aloud, but by the time Peter was three, he was beating me to it. Though he might have been destined for recesses filled with wedgies and swirlies, he is without enemies. The other kids may avoid him, but they are polite enough, the way I am toward my best friend's mother or my teacher. He wears his glasses thick and large, his clothes neat and self-pressed, and carries his only constant companion: a book, any book. And he never complains.

"Goddamn, it's hot!" Betsi announces this to no one in particular. She runs her fingers through her hair, what's left of it, and I wonder if she's forgotten that she chopped it away. Now it's just a dark red eraser on top of a pencil. When she first showed up at the cottage a few days ago, pulling into the driveway in her dusty black Jeep with the top off, I wanted to cry. Her hair had been past her shoulders, thick curling cables, the same color as the wine she used to drink. Betsi didn't seem to notice the look on my face as she bounced over to give me a hug and hand me her bags. I grabbed one of the duffels but couldn't take my eyes off of her. She laughed when she realized why I was frozen, and told me most women kept their hair long simply because boys made them think they'd be ugly without it. She tried to convince me to join her, but I said no way. Then she said I was oppressed, and I said no, actually I was pretty happy, it was just that I liked having braids. Then she sighed so loud her nostrils flared, so I've kept my hair in braids for nearly the entire week just to prove I meant it.

"How many ribs do you want me to save for you, Bets?" Uncle Tim hollers.

"Zero," she yells back. "I think I'm going vegetarian. You've scarred me for life." She nods toward the pig they are holding prisoner.

Uncle Tim laughs. "Coming from the girl who can put down twenty White Castle sliders on her own, I find your statement hard to believe."

"The difference is, no one cooked the cow on a pole in front of me."

"We'd better get this up on the coals," my father interjects.

"Right," Uncle Tim says. "Betsi, if you change your mind, you just let me know."

Barry's still in the lake, practicing flips off the floating diving block in the distance. All of the grandparents—Grandma and Grandpa Dunn, and Dad's mom, Biddie—hover indoors, where the temperature is more forgiving, taking their places around a card table for their usual post-breakfast game of bridge. Mom and my dad's sister, Helen, and her three kids, Kristen, John, and Mark, went into town for groceries to make side dishes for our pigfest, cheesy baked carrots and Caesar salad. Aunt Helen's husband, Richard, her second, stayed only two days because he's a lawyer and he says the courts of justice do not take vacations.

"What a pig." For a second I think Betsi is talking about dinner, which Uncle Tim and Dad have successfully hoisted over the pit and are studying like a painting in a museum. Then behind them I catch the sun bouncing off of something light, a reflection from a mirror, maybe, but it is Barry, shorts pulled down, back turned, aiming his naked ass right at us, a gleaming polished tooth. His body shakes with soundless laughter.

In one flash of motion, Betsi yanks her Michigan State tank top over her head, steps out of her black nylon shorts, and sprints into the lake, her red string bikini wrapped like licorice ropes around her skin. Betsi's slender but swims strong, approaching the diving block in no time, her baby-oiled body melting a path behind her. Barry's swim trunks are now pulled up again and he stands on the far end of the wooden block, smug and sure, arms folded. His skin is the color of cinnamon toast, and long wet locks of black hair fall into his eyes, green as washed sea glass. Just as she reaches the ladder, he dives away on the opposite side, and the water quickly erases all evidence of his entry. Betsi hoists herself up onto the dock, her hair in wet spikes, her chest rising and falling and practically spilling out of her suit. Her cheeks are puffed as if she's holding her breath, but really, they're full of the water she's trying to save until Barry surfaces.

But I don't see him. Not near the diving dock or the buoys or the shore. And when Betsi swallows her ammunition, I know she doesn't see him either. I am about to say something to Dad and Uncle Tim, who are poking the pig with a stick, when I hear a great gasp of water and turn to see Barry shooting up like a geyser behind Betsi. The splash blinds her as he grabs her ankles and pulls her in with him. At first she fights him, spitting water in his face with her yelps and screams, beating on his chest while trying to stay afloat. But then he pulls her to the farthest side of the block, and the splashing and shouting stop. I can't see what they're doing anymore—it's just the water quietly licking the shore—so I skate around to the front and practice Crazy 8's in the driveway while I wait for Mom to come home.

* * * * *

The pig is gone. Its flesh is in the bellies of everyone but me and Betsi, and the parents have taken their swine-filled stomachs to the back porch, protected by screens and surrounded by the zap of the bug light that glows purple and white from where it hangs in the tree. They smoke cigars and sip after-dinner drinks, hot coffee that smells good, like mint, but Mom won't let me have a sip.

After announcing that we ate too late, the grandparents have all gone to bed with a few afghans and comforters added to their sheets, though it's still hovering just below 80 degrees outside. The humidity hangs in the air like a secret. It's hard to make out what is really going on in the thickness of the night.

Barry and Betsi have gone for a walk on the beach. They've been gone for at least an hour, and with Peter's nose buried in another book, I join Kristen, John, and Mark on the floor in the living room. We sprawl out on the shag caramel carpet, studying a game of Pick-Up Sticks. I can still hear the parents' voices on the back porch, puzzle pieces floating in through the window.

"I think she looks good," I hear Mom say.

"Kath. It's only been eight weeks." It's my father's voice.

"So?"

"Well, I just don't want you to get too hopeful. This isn't going to be easy for her," Dad says to Mom, then, "You want me to top that off for you?"

Uncle Tim says, "I'll take some more. I agree with Kath. She looks good, she seems like she's in a good place. She's stronger than you think."

"Your turn, Pres."

"What?" I say, snapping back to the living room.

"Your turn. Come on, hurry up." Kristen wants to win.

Pick-Up Sticks is not my best game. My hands shake even when I'm not trying to move something small and insignificant, and the other kids know this, that I am a weak opponent. I go for what I think is an easy one, the blue stick on the far right, but its neighbors tremble slightly.

John is the first to announce, "You're done. It moved."

"No, it didn't!" I argue, but they have already gone on to the next person. "This is a baby game, I'm not playing anymore," I say as Barry slips inside and Betsi darts upstairs, calling out, "Going to the bathroom!"

"Can I join?" Barry plops down next to me.

"We're in the middle of a game," Kristen tells him. Her thirst for victory is tempered by her concern for the rules and making sure we all know and abide by them.

"Well, me and Pres are partners now, aren't we?" Barry says. He makes me nervous, and I know that it's wrong to feel like that. Not nervous the way Chris Carroll makes me, beautiful Chris Carroll who sat behind me in math and English last year, drawing on the back of my neck with a pencil whenever I wore my hair in a ponytail. It's different than that, like small butterflies tumbling the words in my throat before they can make their way out of my mouth, and by that time, nothing I say makes any sense.

When Barry's around, it's still hard not to think about his mom, even though her funeral was over three years ago. Her name was Marie, and she had the same glass-green eyes as Barry, the same sloping nose. Her hands were thin and delicate but strong, and she used to teach piano and play at every family gathering. Everyone agreed that her pumpkin pie was the best, with just a hint of cinnamon and honey. Mom has been trying to re-create it ever since Aunt Marie died, but it's not the same, though no one will admit it. We add extra Cool Whip and nod and make "mmm" sounds. The pretending has become sort of a family tradition.

At her funeral, Barry wore a tie and sunglasses. He never took them off, not in the church or at Aunt Helen's house afterward. He sat by himself on a bench in Aunt Helen's backyard, and every time someone moved closer to him, Barry would stand up and wander even farther away.

"Let me try," Betsi had told my parents. I had watched as she approached Barry, and I waited for him to shift locations again, but he stayed still, even when she sat down next to him.

8

She held her cigarette pack in her hands and a book of matches, and leaned in closer to Barry to whisper words I couldn't hear. Whatever she said made him smile, then laugh, even if it was just for a minute. Then Betsi struck one of the matches, blew it out, and lit another one. She kept doing this until there were no matches left, and then she pulled out another book from her pocket and handed it to Barry.

"Do-over." It was the only word I could make out as she squeezed the matchbook into his palm, holding on to his hand as she led him back toward the house.

"Thank you," Uncle Tim had mouthed to her from across the room.

She was the only person I saw Barry speak to the entire day.

Everyone had arrived after the service at Aunt Helen's bearing food, cold fried chicken and deli trays and spaghetti casserole. There was also a yellow sheet cake on the table, frosted in sugary white with purple and green flowers, but without a declaration. No "Happy" this or "Congratulations" that, and there were no presents stacked and waiting to be unwrapped. Family and friends milled about the house, with some spilling out onto the back porch to smoke and talk about the cancer and how quickly it had come, and that poor boy and his father, and wasn't it just a beautiful service, and had they tried the cake yet because it was quite good, and who wanted coffee.

"I'm going to get some coffee," Barry announces after he's lead us to victory in the Pick-Up Sticks game.

Kristen's eyes get wide, and she says, "You can't have coffee. That's a grown-up drink." Again with the rules.

Barry laughs. "What do you think I am, a kid? I'm going to be a senior, you know." Kristen looks like she's going to run and tell, because I guess that's what you do when you're ten and all concerned about the rules, but Barry just smiles and pushes himself off the carpet and heads toward the kitchen. Kristen bites her lip and begins to put the game away while John and Mark fight over the television remote, so I'm the only one left. We haven't seen Betsi since she went upstairs. I know she's not on the porch with the parents, because they're telling stories and laughing loudly and I don't hear Betsi's laugh.

I walk past the kitchen on my way to find her. Barry is standing in front of the refrigerator. The glow of the interior fridge light and a little bit of the moon from outside cut across his face, showing me who it is. I wonder if he's looking for milk for his coffee. He still has his swim trunks on and his red hooded football sweatshirt with CAVALIERS and the number 26 on the back. I think about how I will go to the games in the fall with my friends Hannah and Jill and Karen. The older girls sitting in the bleachers with us will squeal about how cute Barry is and try to guess who he will ask to homecoming and even prom. As soon as he makes a touchdown, I'll point him out on the field and tell my friends just loud enough for everyone around us to hear, "Yeah, that's my cousin," as if it's no big deal. And even though I'll be a freshman and he'll be a senior, Barry will invite me and my friends to Telly's for burgers after the game. We'll order salted fries and peanut-fudge sundaes and coffee, of course, and I'll take mine with milk the way Barry does, and one of his friends will say something like "Man, you two really *are* related." Everyone will laugh, and I won't have a curfew because I'm out with family, and when we finally leave at midnight after the restaurant closes, Barry and his friends will give us all a ride home in Uncle Tim's maroon truck that can seat six but we will pile in eight. He'll drop me off last among the girls, get out of the driver's seat to let me out, and hug me good-bye even though his friends are all watching from the truck. The windows will be down, and as I'm walking up to my front door, I'll hear them say, "Your cousin Presley sure is cool."

Barry looks up from the refrigerator and sees me standing in the doorway and says, "You lost?"

"I, uh . . . I'm looking for Betsi."

"Well," he says, looking into the fridge and then back at me, "she's not in here!" He's laughing again.

"Oh, I didn't mean in here. I meant, you know, somewhere in the house." Shut up, shut up, shut up.

"Yeah, I know what you meant." He finds the milk and places the carton on the counter next to his old Boy Scouts mug. "I think she went upstairs."

I nod and scurry out, heading toward Betsi's room. Barry is bunking up with Peter, John is sleeping in the same room as Mark, and I'm stuck with Kristen, but Betsi got her own room, and we were told not to ask why or complain. The door is slightly open and she's got a candle burning next to her bed, a peach votive sitting in a beach shell. The window is half open, with just enough space to crawl through to the overhang, and Betsi is sitting outside on the roof smoking a cigarette in her nylon shorts and a long-sleeved gray T-shirt. She makes a "shhh" motion over her lips and waves for me to sit down next to her. We're right above the parents, but the noise has simmered back down, and it's more difficult to make out their voices.

"I think they've been talking about me," Betsi whispers, and sort of giggles. "But I can't tell for sure. They might be talk-ing about what time everyone is leaving in the morning." Most of us live on the east side of the state, a good five hours from the cottage, and I know we'll leave last because Dad likes to "close up the house," which means I won't be home in time to call Hannah. Betsi hands me her cigarette, but I shake my head.

"Good girl," she says, and takes another drag.

Just before I was born, Betsi convinced Mom to let her name me. Betsi said she had rights because she was Mom's only sister, never mind Dad's siblings. Later, Betsi told me she had pretty much decided on naming me Betsi too, but then Elvis died, and that was when, as Mom puts it, all hell broke loose. Betsi just loved Elvis, I mean really loved him, more than I love raspberry slushes and vanilla-peanut-butter Häagen-Dazs, more than I love Chris Carroll, even more than Mom loves Dad. She says she believed he was on the verge of a big comeback, and she'd saved money from her summer job at the Dairy Queen to buy tickets for a concert, but then he died on the toilet on August 16, 1977, exactly one month before I was born. Mom says Betsi wept for days, and the days turned into weeks, and even when a month had passed and Mom was starting her labor, Betsi was still red-eyed and teary and sad. Mom felt so bad she made good on her promise, so Betsi decided I should keep his memory alive, and that's why she named me Presley.

After Betsi's breakdown, Dad worried she might carry on Elvis's spirit in his other children, a son named The King, or worse yet, a daughter named Priscilla. "It's bad enough I've already got one tainted by her obsessions," he said, and even though I was only two, I knew he was talking about me, and my name, and what it all meant. So Dad put himself in charge, and when my brother was born, he chose the name Peter, which has absolutely nothing to do with Elvis, Priscilla, or Lisa Marie.

"Why are you sneaking a smoke up here?" I ask Betsi as she stubs her cigarette out on the bottom of her tennis shoe.

She shrugs. "Eh, you know how they are," she says. "I don't want anyone to see and start worrying or something. I'm fine."

* * * * *

Here's the thing. I've been told this is "family business," which is just another way of saying a "secret," but Betsi was "sick." That's what Mom and Dad said. Betsi was "sick" and had to go away to this "special hospital where they make you better," and this weekend is the first time any of us have seen her since she went there. With all the cryptic speak, at first I didn't understand exactly what was wrong with Betsi and I panicked, asking Mom if she was sick like Aunt Marie. Mom said, "No, no, no," and sighed. She said sometimes people get sad or mad and do things that are bad for their body, like eat too much or drink too much. Mom said this was more like the drink-too-much kind, and Betsi had to go to this place where she learned how to control that. Why Mom didn't just come out and say Betsi had a drinking problem, I don't know. I guess my family has a tendency to choose the words they think sound the best versus just telling it like it is.

I didn't remember Betsi being sad or mad, I just remember she always had a glass of red wine in her hand and seemed to fall asleep at family gatherings if she came alone, or she'd show up really late, talking very fast, with lots of different guys. Bo was a car salesman who had two kids and an ex-wife he called The Fish. Then there was Roger, who had tattoos of skulls and snakes and drove up to our house with Betsi on the back of his motorcycle, neither of them wearing helmets. The last one was Eddie, who had big hard arms and talked mostly about the

Detroit Lions and drank his beer from cans, popping off the tabs in some sort of special way, and then handing them to Betsi and saying, "That's for later," and wink. No one liked Eddie very much. I could tell that from the way Mom talked through her teeth to him and Dad always found some sort of garage project to escape to when they'd stop by. Eddie wasn't very cute and he seemed way too old, and I couldn't figure out why Betsi hung out with him because I was certain she was very pretty. This was back when her hair was still long, and whenever she'd take me to the mall, guys would always end up following us around or make up stupid reasons to come talk to her, like asking her where did she get that shirt or did she have the time.

Anyway, Eddie was the last one, at the beginning of summer, and I'm still not sure what happened with him, but it must have been serious, because Betsi showed up at our house really late one weeknight. Dad didn't have summers off like we do, and he had to go to work early. I think it was a Tuesday, and when I heard all the noise downstairs, first our doorbell ringing again and again and again, then the heavy footsteps on our stairs, then the voices, I tried to come down too, but Mom snapped at me to go back to bed and I knew she meant it. Before I turned around, I saw Betsi with Mom on the couch while Dad paced in front of the two of them. Betsi was crying and holding her arm, and even though I was only there for a few seconds, I could see some sort of bluish marks because she was wearing a tank top and Mom had flipped the light on in the living room. Betsi was sort of talking, but her words were all slurred like when you're crying really hard and nothing comes out right. Before I closed my bedroom door, I heard Dad say, "That's it, Betsi. You're going to get some help. You're just as bad as he is, and being around that asshole has made it worse. You've got to stop." Hearing my dad say "asshole" made my stomach hurt, because he doesn't swear unless something is very, very wrong.

The next morning Betsi was nowhere to be found and it was as though it had never happened, except Mom made a lot of muffled phone calls. Before Peter and I were allowed to go to the park pool, she sat us down and explained about the "family business" and that we probably wouldn't see Betsi until the reunion at the cottage but that everything was absolutely fine. Then she gave us five extra dollars to spend at the pool concession stand and sent us on our way.

* * * * *

Betsi taps out another cigarette and shoves the pack down the front of her shirt into the strap of her bikini. She pulls a lighter out of her pocket and gets a flame on the first try. The exhale floats over her head as she lies down on her back, stretching her arms above her head and her legs out, pointing her flip-flopped toes. I lie down next to her, staring up at the sky that seems different from the one at home, because out here there are so many stars I never get to see. Just then one streaks across the sky, and I say, "Did you see—" and Betsi says, "Yeah. Wow," and I love that we both saw it at the same time, just the two of us.

Betsi says, "I'm going to go home with you guys for a little while. Did your mom tell you that?" Mom did tell us that, me and Peter, just a few days ago, but she also told us to not make a big deal out of anything to Betsi and to "give her a break." I'm not sure what qualifies as a big deal, so I just say, "Hmm," and dig into my pocket for my cherry lip balm. Betsi reaches out her hand and I pass the tube to her when I'm done. She rubs it slowly on her lips, still looking up at the sky, and says, "You know what I missed most when I was at the clinic? My music. That's the first thing I did when I left. Got in my Jeep and popped in one of my Elvis tapes and just sat there and turned it up real loud and listened before I even left the parking lot." She takes another drag, the smoke dancing slowly from her lips. "One of these days, we're going to Graceland, Presley. You and I." She places the lip balm in my palm, and I pull off the cap like I'm going to put more on too, but I just smell the top, cherry and wax and her nicotine, and wonder if people named after the King are allowed into Graceland for free.

Chapter 2

The First Day of School

Most firefighters smoke. This is what I learn after the first day of school, not in class but standing in front of our house just before midnight. I guess it makes sense when I think about what they're around all day, like if I worked at the Magdalena bakery, I'd probably eat a lot of lemon poppy-seed cake and caramel bars. None of the firefighters smoke in our house, but as soon as they get outside, and as long as they're not unraveling hoses, the soft crumpled foil packs come out from the pockets of their long, heavy tan coats. They use matchbooks instead of lighters and take quick puffs to bring the cigarettes down to filters in just a matter of minutes. Maybe it's because they never know when they'll have to drop everything and go. When they're finished, the firefighters toss the butts in the street, extinguishing them with their black boots, but then pick them up to dispose of elsewhere. They never leave any evidence behind.

I also learn that firefighters like to tell you the good news first. "The good news is, the entire house didn't burn down" and "The good news is, there were alarms installed to warn you." It's the fire chief who makes these statements to Mom and Dad, a man named Meyer, according to the tag on his coat, with gray temples and a matching thick mustache. I guess it's his turn to smoke as I watch him strike the match by folding the cover back with his wide, callused hands and dirty fingernails. He offers his pack to Mom and Dad, who shake their heads, and the chief nods, his cigarette dangling out of the corner of his mouth as he gives them the alternative. "Detectors are crucial. Without them, it could've been a lot worse."

Below me, the pavement is still damp from a late-evening shower, the humid air swimming underneath the glow of the streetlights. None of us have shoes on, and because of this, Mom tells us to stay on the grass, but she and Dad are both pacing on the sidewalk and too busy and distracted to notice if we're following their orders. There are a lot of emergency vehicles for what seems like a false alarm—the fire truck, two police cars, even an ambulance that's pulling away after determining that no one was seriously hurt. The sirens are all silent but the lights are still on, circling swashes of blue and red dancing across the white panels of our house. Peter is on the grass underneath a tree, with his book and a flashlight he managed to grab from his nightstand before we fled, reading as though he's still in bed and leaning against his headboard.

Betsi is perched on the curb, her knees tucked underneath her chin, wearing forest-green boxers and a matching tank top. The officers have been clustering around her since they got here, asking if she'd like some coffee from a silver thermos or a smoke, which she accepts from a burly firefighter named Fisher. Mom and Dad are still talking to the chief while Betsi rocks on the curb, puffing on the donated cigarette and flicking it after each drag, which is odd, because usually she'll let it grow a bit, like a fingernail. From the outside, the house looks exactly the same, except for all the trucks and cruisers and siren lights.

"How is it?" Dad asks the chief.

"Not bad. Not bad at all," he says, wiping a tiny smudge off his brow. By now most of the neighbors who were gathered on their front stoops underneath their porch lights have retreated to the safety of their homes. "Mostly it's just smoke damage to the den on the first floor. Looks like it started in there, near the window." The chief catches my eye as I peek from behind Dad's shoulder. "You mind if I talk to you privately?" he says, motioning my parents toward the street with his metal hat.

"Of course," Dad answers, and he and Mom follow the chief to a spot too far away for me to hear what's being said. I stay on the grass like I'm supposed to, but as close to the sidewalk as possible, watching Mom and Dad nod repeatedly at the chief's words. Then Dad shakes the chief's hand and turns around, his eyes scanning the front yard for his target. It's as if Mom can sense what's coming, because she's on Dad's heels as soon as he finds it and storms over. She follows him like a little dog, yapping "No" and "Don't" and "Just don't." Dad ignores her as he reaches Betsi, yanking the cigarette out of her hand. He tosses it into the street and lifts her up by her elbow, his voice low but sharp, serious. "You see what you've done? You see what could have happened?"

Betsi shakes herself loose from Dad's grip with a "Don't touch me!" so shrill it startles the cluster of officers who are gathering up their things. Her breathing flutters, but as she backs away from Dad, her voice returns strong, her words anchored. "It started in my room. That doesn't mean it was my fault. I wasn't smoking in the house. I do not smoke in your fucking house."

"Betsi!" Mom scolds, shooting a look of embarrassment at the officers, as though she's invited them over for lemonade or a barbecue or Christmas dinner. Dad's hands are on his hips and he's shaking his head slowly, as if he's trying to work a kink out of his neck. Mom wedges herself between them ever so slightly, her eyes darting back and forth like she can't make up her mind.

Finally Dad lets out a loud, slow sigh. "It wasn't a cigarette. It was the candle. It started from a candle left burning. In the den."

After that, no one says a word: not Betsi, not Dad, not Mom, not the firefighters or the officers, not Peter, and definitely not me. All I can hear are the garbled electronic messages coming through the police scanners of other emergencies nearby, situations that require backup and assistance. We all stand completely still for a moment that feels like an hour until Dad breaks the spell and says to Mom without looking at Betsi, "Take everyone inside and pack a few things. We shouldn't stay in the house tonight. I'll wrap things up out here."

Betsi opens her mouth, her breath drawing into her lungs as if she has something else to say, but nothing comes out. It's just her lips parted, open, waiting to explain. Instead she turns and begins heading toward the house. Peter has stayed underneath the tree this entire time, and he shines his flashlight from his book to her feet as she walks. The spotlight guides her back inside, leaves and twigs sticking to her heels, her soles dirty from the pavement.

* * * * *

The first day of school begins like this. My alarm goes off at 7:00 A.M. because as a freshman I have the responsibility of reporting to class by 8:15 rather than 8:35. I spent most of last night staring at my clock radio, the digital numbers eventually a blur, my mind racing with thoughts of losing my way within the new halls I'd toured only once, last May. Today is crucial. With it come the pictures for our school ID, the same photo that will appear in the yearbook handed out in June. What happens today will be the image I carry with me for the rest of the school year, the rest of my high school life, maybe longer, maybe forever.

I'm standing in the bathroom between my room and the den, where Betsi has been sleeping since we returned from the cottage last weekend. I'm wearing my favorite lime-green underwear, which I just noticed has a tear around the waistband. My matching T-shirt already has sweat rings underneath the arms, even though I've applied three coats of deodorant, and it will just get worse when I get to school, where only one building of three is air-conditioned. I pour gobs of pink gel into my hands, then coat not just my hair but the mirror and my shoulders with a can of my mother's White Rain. I even steal a few squirts of Betsi's mousse in a last-ditch effort to try and make something hold. Under this recipe of so many products, my hair is limp and frizzy and wet. Even though I spent an hour on the phone with Hannah last night, none of the predetermined outfits are working. It's too warm for my new fall plaid skirt and navy cardigan, and the backup outfit cobbled together from my summer clothes, a wraparound pin-striped skirt and the T-shirt I'm sweating circles into, feels worn and tired. I also woke up this morning with a huge red bump on my chin that's too new to come to a head, and my makeup looks like orange paint on top of it.

It's 7:24 A.M. When I realize Hannah and her mom will be here to pick me up in under thirty minutes, I begin to cry.

Dad had left for work before I got out of the shower, like he always does, in his suit and the blue-and-red-striped tie we gave him last Father's Day. Mom is downstairs making breakfast, not for me, because I lie and say I eat it at school. It's for Peter, who's starting fifth grade. He's become the senior of elementary school and is concerned only with who he has for math and whether his eggs are scrambled hard. He came out of the bathroom just as I was waiting to go in, and I swear he had on the same blue-jean shorts he wore yesterday when he rode his bike down to the lake to "pre-read" for school. How do you pre-read for fifth grade? The truth is, I'm jealous, because I'd rather be starting fifth grade than ninth grade. There's no rank in ninth grade. It all lies back at my middle school, where some seventh-grader has taken my place.

My high school brings together not just the eighth-graders from my old school, but those from another public school, two privates, and one Catholic. In my middle school, I ran with the in-betweens. The cool kids didn't pick on us, but they weren't exactly inviting us to their pool parties either. The nerdy kids worried about the cool kids, and back then, we in-betweens would offer them an occasional hello and smile because most of us went to catechism and were taught to treat others the way you'd want to be treated. The in-between isn't a bad place to be, but when systems are combined from four or five other places, that rank could easily get bumped down a few notches. There's only so much room at the top, and only so much room below, and it's not going to improve my chances if I don't figure out how to stop sweating, how to get dressed, how to move on.

Even though I've tried to be quiet since I started crying, I hear Betsi shuffling out of her room. It's an important day for her as well. Dad called in a favor with a friend of his at a car dealership and set her up with an interview for a receptionist position. "It doesn't pay much," Dad had warned, "but it's a start." Her appointment isn't until 11:30. I know this because Mom has taped reminder notes on the refrigerator, the television, even the bathroom mirror. I hear Betsi tap on the door with two quick knocks. Before I can wipe my face, she slips inside. She's got one of Mom's robes wrapped around her, the white silk kimono, and her cropped hair is sprouting in six different directions. She glances at me and then turns on the faucet, reaching for her blue toothbrush. We all have colors assigned to us, but Mom always keeps an extra stock of blues that mean "guest."

"What's wrong?" Betsi asks with her mouth full of toothpaste, foaming white in the corners. My crying has become a series of short sniffs as I point to my hair and then my chin, and Betsi says nothing but nods, spitting into the sink and tapping her brush on the side. She leaves the faucet running and grabs one of the hand towels, then gets the shampoo and conditioner from the shower stall. She adjusts the knobs and tests the water with her wrists, motioning for me to lean over the sink.

"We don't have enough time—" I begin, but Betsi shushes me and guides my head under the water, which is exactly the right temperature, just like at the hair salon. Her fingertips work in slow circles at first, scrubbing out the overload of beauty products, her nails scratching my scalp lightly. It is just a matter of minutes before the conditioner is rinsed and she's rubbing my head with the towel hard enough so that when she lifts it, my hair feels almost dry.

Betsi sits me on the toilet lid again with the towel draped around my shoulders. She takes a tissue and wipes off the makeup and then pulls out her floral bag from underneath the sink. It's overflowing with slick tubes and compacts and brushes, and she rubs something on my chin that stings a bit, then a cool light cream all over my face. She studies as she paints, working quickly with small brushes and telling me to close my eyes while she blows lightly on my lids, her breath still minty. She turns me around and runs a pick through my hair to get the snags out, squeezing just a quarter-size dollop of gel into her hands, massaging it into my hair and scalp. "Don't dry it. It'll just get frizzy," she says, and I nod, biting my lip so I won't start crying again. "They still take yearbook pictures on the first day?" she asks, and I nod again. "Bastards." It makes me giggle. "You know, Presley, I was in high school not that long ago. I mean, honestly, I bet I could get dressed and go with you and pass for a senior." She steps back to survey her work.

"Barry's a senior," I say.

"Hm-mm," Betsi says. "Okay. Good. Now, what are you wearing?" I point to the wraparound skirt crumpled in the corner. "Oh no," she says, shaking her head. "Come with me."

        ★ ★ ★ ★ ★

Even though I know it's coming, I blink at the photographer's flash, and I'm certain he has captured me with my eyes half closed. Mr. Lyndon, the gym teacher, stands guard off to one side near the exit in his blue and red tracksuit, and he hands me a numbered receipt with my name on it as I walk away. "Stay out of trouble, Moran," he warns. No matter what school or grade, the gym teachers always call me by my last name.

Hannah is waiting for me at the door, waving with one hand and holding her books against her chest with the other. "How did that go?" she asks, her blond hair cascading down her shoulders, her pink sundress still perfectly crisp, as if it has just been ironed.

"I think it will make a great 'before' shot."

"Oh, come on! I bet it's not as bad as you think. You look really cute today!" she adds. I'm not so sure. Betsi did save my face and hair, but she insisted I wear one of her denim miniskirts with a black tank top. The waist feels snug, and I keep tugging at the hem, as if I can make it grow longer.

"*You* look cute today," I tell her, which is true but not much different from every day for Hannah. "That's new, right?" I ask, pointing at her dress.

"Yes, but it was on sale." Hannah's parents are both lawyers with their own firms. They live in the west end of town, where the houses are three or four times the size of those in my neighborhood. She's an only child, like Barry, but Hannah's parents buy her clothes as if she has siblings to receive the hand-me-downs. I don't think most of the kids we go to school with know how well off she is, and I'm one of only a few girls who has actually seen her closets—all three of them.

"Are you coming over for dinner tonight?" I ask. Hannah eats at our house at least twice a week; she insists these are the only nights she doesn't end up with a carton of moo-shu pork while her parents prepare for morning depositions.

"Maybe," she says. "My mother thinks I need to be more considerate—her word, not mine—now that Betsi is staying at your house again."

"It's not permanent," I explain. "I'll see you at lunch?" We've compared class schedules, and besides lunch, we have just fifth-period math in common. I'll reunite with Mr. Lyndon in gym class during the last period of the day, but Hannah is stuck with him during third.

"You're so lucky to have gym class last," she tells me again. "You can go to class and not worry about what you look like after—you can just leave and go home."

I shrug. No matter what period gym class is, it's still the class I dread the most. Today we're on what they call an "amended" bell schedule to make time for the pictures, so I've got seven minutes instead of nine to get to my first class, English.

"See you at lunch!" Hannah says, disappearing into the wave of students flooding the hallway.

My English class is on the second floor in the main building, and I'm forced to walk down the hallway with the senior lockers, which are twice as wide as those assigned to freshmen. Even without the location to tip me off, the seniors are easy to identify. The girls move with a certain confidence, their shirts a little bit too tight, their lipstick bright and eyes teasing with coats of mascara. The senior boys have broad shoulders to hold up varsity jackets that glitter with championship pins, their cheeks freshly shaved and threatening to grow stubble by 2:00 P.M. They also look misplaced, too old for this school but too young for suits and ties.

I'm trying to remember if my class is in room 206 or 260, neither of which seems to exist, when I feel a hand on my shoulder. "Hey, Pres."

"Hey, Barry." He's carrying just a blue ballpoint pen with the cap missing, and there's a tall boy standing next to him, smirking from underneath a mop of curly brown hair.

"You talking to freshmen now?" the boy says.

"This is my cousin, asshole."

"Oh, well, excuse me."

"Presley, this is Jack."

"Hi," I say. I didn't recognize him at first. I don't think I've seen Jack since Aunt Marie's funeral, and I remember him much shorter, with round, bulky glasses. "We've met before," I remind him.

Jack says nothing, leaning against the locker, examining his fingernails.

"So who'd you get stuck with for algebra?" Barry says.

I pause. "Overwood?"

"Overwood? Who's Overwood?" Jack barges in, laughing and picking at something underneath his thumbnail.

"Um, I mean—"

"You mean *Under*wood?" He's still laughing.

"Yeah, that's what I meant." I can already feel new sweat seeping under my armpits.

"Oh, man, don't tell him you're related to me!" Barry says, taking a light green apple out of his front pocket. He dusts it off on his T-shirt and takes a bite. There's a group of older girls making their way down the hallway, and they throw out a collective "Hiiiii Barry!" as they approach. He grins and gives them a two-finger wave with the hand holding the apple. The tallest one in the center of the cluster stops directly in front of Barry.

"Nice tan, Barry." Her wavy chestnut hair is tied loosely at the nape of her neck with a white grosgrain ribbon.

"Oh, thanks, Liz. Where are you off to?"

"French. I'm taking AP this year." She's at least four inches taller than I am. Her eyes dart to me, and I notice she's wearing pale gold eye shadow. I look down at the linoleum floor and fidget on the heels of my sandals.

"This is my cousin Presley," Barry tells her.

"She's a freshman," Jack adds.

"I can see that," Liz says in a very matter-of-fact voice. She turns her attention back to Barry. "Give me a call later, okay?"

"Uh, sure," Barry tells her. "See you." The girls begin moving in their swarm again, buzzing with whispers and a sprinkling of giggles.

"Is that your girlfriend?" I ask as soon as she's out of earshot.

Jack snorts. "He wishes."

"More like *you* wish," Barry throws at Jack. "She's just a friend." He takes another bite of his apple. "So," he says, chewing, "Betsi still at your house?"

"Yeah."

"I thought she was getting her own place."

"She is . . . I think. Eventually. She has a job interview today."

"She get it?"

"I don't know. It's not until eleven-thirty."

"I bet she gets it. She's like that."

"Yeah, I guess," I say, tugging once more on the denim, which is suffocating me.

"So where are you going?" Jack interrupts again, apparently bored with his hands.

"I have English. Room two-oh-six. Or two-sixty."

"Davidson?" he asks. I nod. "It's over there." Jack motions across the hall, toward a door with the number 216 above it. "We could get you a map if you want."

"Shut up," Barry says, and then turns back to me. "You'd better get to class."

He waves and shoves Jack down the hallway, which is now nearly empty. As the bell rings, right before I walk into the room, I hear Jack say, "Nice skirt," and then they turn the corner and disappear.

★ ★ ★ ★ ★

Class after class, it's the same question: "Are you related to Barry Moran?"

"Yes, that's my cousin."

"Yes, he's my cousin."

"We're cousins."

The reactions vary only slightly.

"Well, I hope you take to algebra a little faster than he did!"

"Well, I hope you take to English as well as he did!"

"Well, I hope you pay attention to history the same way he did!"

★ ★ ★ ★ ★

When I get to my last class of the day, there's a note taped to the girls' locker-room door that tells us to report directly to the main gym. We cluster on the shiny wood floor in between the colored bars and circles that mark the basketball court. As Mr. Lyndon announces that today will be a review of practices and procedures, I spot Chris Carroll standing underneath the net with two other boys. I haven't seen him since eighth-grade graduation last year. Hannah told me she heard his family spent the entire summer up north at their cottage, which unfortunately is nowhere near ours. He's still tan, and he's wearing a gray T-shirt and canvas shorts. His legs are hairy, like a man's. He smiles, not at me but at something funny his friend says, and I gasp. His braces are off too. But then I realize this is not a class where he's going to sit behind me and draw on my neck; in this class, Chris Carroll is going to see me sweat. Mr. Lyndon hands us a stack of papers: a permission slip that waives the school's responsibility in case of an injury, a reminder to buy a personal lock, a form to order a uniform. I grab a copy of each sheet as it passes and consider running from the room, from Chris, from the polyester shorts and boxy T-shirts that await me. But I'm surrounded, unable to move, and Mr. Lyndon seems to be directing every comment directly at me. "In this class, I expect a hundred percent effort, all the time," and because I can't escape his stare, I nod quietly and stay planted.

After the last bell, I gather up my things at my locker, shoving the papers and my math book into my backpack. Math is the only homework assigned on the first day. Mom is scheduled to pick me up near the bike racks and I wait with Hannah, who is going to a meeting about cheerleading tryouts at 3:30 P.M.

"So Carroll is in your gym class this year?" Hannah says, offering me a stick of cherry-flavored gum.

"Yes. I'm doomed," I tell her, unwrapping the silver foil and popping the piece into my mouth. "For real. Doomed."

"Oh, Pres. I'm so sorry." Normally Hannah takes the "glass is half full" approach, but we're talking about gym class here— horrible uniforms, team selections, sweat. Running. Sweat. Oh God.

"Why couldn't I have been given the gift of athletic coordination, like you? And we could *both* be going to cheerleading tryouts right now."

"Eh, I'm probably just going to make an ass out of myself. I can barely do the splits. This team is way more serious than warming the sidelines at a middle school basketball game." She checks her watch and grabs her bag. "I'll call you when I get home!" she yells, half walking, half running toward the gym. Even now she looks graceful.

My mother pulls up a few minutes later. Betsi is sitting in the front seat, and Peter is in the back. I forgot he gets picked up first now.

"How'd it go? How'd it go?" Betsi asks, practically bouncing out of her seat as I open the back door.

"Okay," I say. She continues staring at me, waiting for more of an answer. "My math teacher seems like a jerk."

"Who do you have?" she asks.

"Underwood."

"Oh God, is he still there? He must be a hundred years old!" She laughs.

"Barry had him too," I say.

"Did you see him today?" Mom asks.

"Yeah, in the morning."

"Oh yeah?" Betsi says, still turned around in her seat. "What'd he have to say?"

"Not much. He asked about you. I told him about the interview—" I realize what she's been waiting for. "Oh my God, what happened?"

I can see Mom smiling as Betsi begins to relate the details. "I don't know for sure yet, but they said they'd call. I think they liked me. It's a really nice dealership, and I'd have my own little area and desk. There's a mall nearby where I can go on my lunch breaks, and of course once I save up, I'd get a great deal on a car."

"Betsi, don't get too ahead of yourself," Mom says, turning onto our street.

"I know, I know. But I have a *really* good feeling about this." Betsi finally faces front in her seat, singing quietly to herself until we pull into the driveway, and it's not even an Elvis song on the radio.

As soon as we walk inside, the phone rings, and Betsi squeals, but Mom says, "Let me get it, let me get it. You don't want to seem too desperate." She picks up the receiver and says "Hello" and "Yes, I'll get her," then passes the phone to Betsi.

Betsi plays the game-show host. "This is Betsi Dunn. Yes. I see. Thank you *so* much for calling." When she hangs up, we're all holding our breath, even Peter, who hasn't said a word since I got into the car. Betsi smiles and says, "They want me to start Monday."

We're all jumping up and down as if we've won the lottery. Mom says we can order Giacomo's to celebrate, a treat we never get unless it's a birthday or sleepover, but she adds, "This is a special circumstance."

The phone rings again, and this time Betsi answers it first. She rounds the corner with the phone, her voice lowered, the white spiral cord stretching as she moves farther away from us. Mom pulls out the menu for Giacomo's from the junk drawer and hands it to me for review. The plan is to call Dad at work with the order so he can pick it up on the way home. Betsi comes back into the kitchen a few minutes later and places the phone in the cradle. "I have to go," she says, her voice calmer and more subdued.

"What do you mean? We're just about to order," Mom says.

"I . . . I have a meeting. Save some for me?" she asks, and Mom nods. Betsi grabs her purse and keys from the kitchen table, waving as she heads out the door.

"She has a work meeting already?" I ask, clutching the menu in my hands.

Mom shakes her head. "No. She's meeting . . . I think she probably had to go meet some friends from her clinic."

"Why?" I ask, trying to force my mother to stop dancing around with her delicate words.

"Did you pick out what you want?" Mom says, ignoring me and turning to load the dishwasher. "Hurry up. I need to catch your father before he leaves."

Later, we feast on a Veggie Delight, Chicago-style, with bread sticks and salad and even cups of Italian ice for dessert. After I finish my math homework, Mom says we can watch television. We sit in the family room, Mom and Dad on the couch, Peter and me sprawled on the floor. At 10:00 P.M., Mom goes into the kitchen and opens the oven, where she's kept the pizza warm since dinner. She pulls out foil, wraps the leftover slices, and places them in the refrigerator.

"Should we leave the door unlocked?" Mom asks Dad from the kitchen.

"No," he says, folding the evening paper in half. "She has a key." He turns off the television and says to Peter and me, "Time for bed."

* * * * *

I wake up to voices outside my door, and then the ceiling light switches on abruptly and Dad is shaking my shoulders, saying, "Come with me." I try to grab my shoes, but he says,

33

"There's no time," and picks me up so my feet don't touch the ground, which he hasn't done since I was very young.

The hallway smells like smoke, not like Betsi's cigarettes but like campfire, like burnt toast. My eyes itch and I can't see anything. Dad takes the stairs in what seems like one leap and then we are outside in the night air, Dad still holding on to me, Mom holding on to Peter, Betsi holding on to herself, the sound of sirens approaching in the distance.

* * * * *

The Parkcrest Motel is only fifteen minutes away, off of I-696. The room has two queen beds and a rollaway. Dad refused to pay for two separate rooms, so he and Mom will share one bed, Betsi and I the other, and Peter will sleep on the rollaway. He's already brushed his teeth, set his glasses carefully next to the lamp on the nearest table, and tucked himself underneath the white sheets and spongy mustard-colored blanket. There's no comforter on the rollaway, and I ask Peter if he wants ours, but he doesn't answer, his eyelids tight as if he's already asleep. Maybe he is.

A card folded into a triangle on top of the TV declares FREE HBO, but Mom shakes her head and mumbles, "Not now," when I reach for the remote that's Velcroed to the top. After that, no one talks. We each take a turn in the brightly lit bathroom, with the toilet seat sanitized, the roll of paper folded into a triangle at the end like a bandana, and rough white towels stacked overhead on a silver rack. I count only four but decide to wait until morning to point this out to Mom. She's already called the message center at both my school and Peter's, explaining a "slight family emergency" that will keep us out until noon or so.

Betsi uses the bathroom last. The rest of us just washed our faces and brushed our teeth, but she turns on the tub, the water harsh and forceful. When I don't hear the stopper pulled, I think she must be sitting on the edge and rinsing the dirt off her feet. Mom and Dad get into their bed before Betsi finishes. I wait in mine, concentrating on the digital alarm clock. This one has red numbers instead of green, like the one I have at home, and just like last night, I watch the time turn from 1:26 to 1:34. At 1:44, Betsi finally emerges. She smells like bar soap when she slides under the covers next to me, and I don't know whether I should say anything or pretend I am asleep like everyone else. We're both lying on our backs, faces toward the ceiling. I can hear her sniffing just slightly, so I reach toward her and find her hands clasped on top of her belly. When I take one of hers to hold with my own, it's shaking. I tighten my grip and she squeezes back. The room is silent except for her muffled cry and the whir of the radiator that sits underneath the window by the door. I keep holding Betsi's hand, which is delicate but warm, and soon I can't tell the difference between hers and my own. My eyes are closed, and it feels like I am falling into my pillow when I hear Betsi whisper, "Presley?"

I turn toward her, catching part of her face in the sliver of moonlight coming in through a crack in the heavy paisley drapes. Her pupils are large and wet, like shiny beetles. "Presley," she whispers again. "Have you ever looked back on something and thought if you could just hit rewind or call a do-over, you could make things right?" I watch the water in her eyes run over, gently falling toward her mouth. "I feel like that every day of my life."

"But it was an accident. You didn't mean for it to happen." I wonder if my parents are still awake.

"I think I might destroy everything I touch," she says, biting on her lower lip.

I pause, then squeeze our clasped hands underneath the blankets and say, "Not everything."

She nods, and we fall asleep like this, facing each other and holding the proof between us for now.

Chapter 3

Happy Birthday to Me

The Sunday before my fourteenth birthday, Mom and
Betsi are outside preparing the garden for the fall. Actually, it's
Mom doing most of the gardening while Betsi leans on a shovel
nearby. Every once in a while, Betsi moves around the piles of
dirt in front of her, reshaping them into one large mound, then
into three separate smaller hills, and then into a flat pancake. But
it's not really changing anything, like when I push my vegeta-
bles around on my dinner plate. No matter how many times I
arrange them, they're still there, waiting to be dealt with. I'm
supposed to be outside helping too, but Mom decided my math
homework was more important. It's spread out on the kitchen
table next to my calculator and textbook. But algebra can wait. I

perch on the kitchen counter near the sink, peeking through the yellow curtains into the backyard.

September isn't even over, but autumn has crept in quickly and kissed the trees, the leaves stained with gold and rust. Some years we don't switch the sheets from cotton to flannel until Halloween or later; this year the weather is predicted to turn cold early. Mom kneels on a foam cushion in front of her garden, which holds the remnants of snap peas and baby tomatoes and a patch of mint. Her hands are covered in gardening gloves to protect her from sticks and thorns.

Their conversation floats in through the window, cranked open for the crisp fall air. "I can tell he wants me to go," I hear Betsi say, resting the shovel against the wheelbarrow, tired of pretending. The "he" is Dad, who left twenty minutes ago for the hardware store to get one more can of Oyster Shell #4143. After the new carpet that went in last week and the final coat of paint, all of the damage to the den will have been repaired. Betsi moved into my room after the fire, though I never see her. I just hear her, either leaving early in the morning for work or coming in late at night after one of her meetings. Sometimes when she gets back, it's so late that it's almost time for me to get up for school, but more often than not, she's also crying—small, brief whimpers—and that's when I lie as still as possible. I offered to let Betsi sleep in my bed with me but she set up an air mattress on the floor and told me this was all just temporary. It's been a little over two weeks, and as far as I'm concerned, she can stay in my room forever. Just this morning I found her at the kitchen table, her head in one hand, the other clutching a fat red marker and circling apartment ads, the ink so thick it's bled through the other side.

"He wants me to go, doesn't he?" Betsi repeats.

Mom pauses, and I can see the silhouette of her sigh in the cold air. "No, he doesn't."

Betsi pulls a cigarette and lighter from the pocket of her puffy baby-blue vest. I don't see the look Mom gives her, but I hear Betsi say, "What? I'm not anywhere near the house."

Mom goes back to her business in the garden bed. "Betsi. You can't possibly afford anything on your own yet. Just give it some time, save some money from your job. We can look after the holidays."

Sometimes when I hear Mom talking to Betsi, it sounds more like mother to daughter than sibling to sibling, but I've seen photos of them together when they've seemed more sisterly. My favorite is from a neighborhood Christmas party when my mother was just out of high school. Betsi must have been my age, and she has shiny red tinsel wrapped around her neck like a boa. Both of them have strips of frosty white eye shadow swept across their lids. They are in party dresses, laughing, my mother toasting the room with her champagne glass. I don't think I've ever seen her drink champagne or even wine, but I like looking at proof that she used to celebrate. A few nights ago, I showed Betsi the photo again, and she had the same reaction she always does—"That's the night your mother met your father"—despite the fact that he's not even in the picture.

"No one wants you to leave," Mom says. Betsi snorts. "It was an accident," Mom reminds her. It's been said so many times, over the phone, to my friends at school, to the neighbors we bump into at the grocery store, it's as if the words have lost meaning or become a foreign language. They're a secret code, a gathering blur of meaningless letters we continue to say over and over again because they're what we need to believe.

"Well, it doesn't feel like an accident. He's acting like I

killed someone," Betsi says, carefully ashing her cigarette into the swirl of coffee turned cold in the bottom of her mug.

"Betsi, don't be so melodramatic," Mom says, checking her watch, but I think she knows Betsi's right, in a way. Dad hasn't actually spoken to Betsi since that night.

I duck down beneath the curtain to avoid being spotted. Mom's already set out the ingredients for tonight's dinner—a can of stewed tomatoes, garlic powder, bread crumbs, a package of ground beef defrosting on a plate. Her meat loaf takes over an hour to prepare and cook, but the house fills with a smell that is rich and spicy. It's almost better than the actual meal. It's a smell that makes me forget anything is wrong until I get to the table and the plates of food are passed around wordlessly.

"Maybe I should go stay at Barry and Tim's," Betsi says, leaning against the garage, her cheeks flushed, fingers clutching the last puffs of her cigarette.

Mom stops pulling the weeds into the neat cluster next to her. "That's not necessary. But you'd better put out that cigarette before he gets home." Betsi drops the butt into the mug, while Mom stays perfectly balanced on her knees and continues to remove what doesn't belong, salvaging what she can before the air shifts without warning one night soon and ruins everything.

* * * * *

On Friday, the day of my sleepover, Betsi and I make plans to pick up the last item for the party—my birthday cake. I feel too old to be calling it a sleepover, so I've been telling people, "I've got some people coming over," like Betsi says when she's going to meet friends from her group. I remind Chris Carroll of this as we stand in line during basketball drills in gym class, thinking this bit of information might intrigue him enough to ask more details. Instead he just leans down and tightens his laces. "For my birthday," I add.

"Hannah coming?" he asks, standing back up. I nod and get a final statement of "Sounds cool" before Mr. Lyndon blows his whistle, which means it's Chris's turn for a layup. I also invited Jill and Karen, whom I've known since fourth grade. This is the group I eat my lunch with, though I like Hannah the best, probably because I've known her longest. Jill is a pro at any sport and doesn't care if she trips, sweats, or falls. She likes to tell us the jokes she hears from the kids she babysits: "Why did the tissue dance? Because it had a little boogie in it!" And she never seems to get upset about anything—boys, grades, her parents, none of it. She just shrugs and recycles another G-rated joke. Karen, on the other hand, has faked illness to get out of gym more than anyone I know. She always seems bored and spends a lot of time talking about what she'd rather be doing, like visiting her aunt in New York City. But she's fiercely loyal, and the boys shake around her, with her cabaret legs and slinky eyes, so she's a powerful addition to the group.

Betsi has negotiated a half-day with her dealership, claiming she has a doctor's appointment. I wait for her at the side stoop by the senior parking lot, my school bag at my feet and my English assignment on my lap—*The Great Gatsby*. I am working my way through another one of Jay Gatsby's legendary parties when I hear the doors open behind me and a flurry of strong denim-covered legs file by. One pair stops, and I look up to see Barry. "Hey. You need a ride?"

"Hey. Uh. No. Betsi is coming to get me," I stammer, trying to hide the book so it doesn't look like I'm doing homework.

"Really?" Barry asks, almost like he thinks I'm lying. "Isn't she working?"

"She took a half-day," I explain. Like Barry, most of his friends are wearing Cavalier varsity jackets because there's a game tomorrow afternoon. Jack doesn't wear school colors, let alone a varsity jacket—he doesn't play football—but he's the only one who lingers while Barry's teammates scatter to their cars.

Jack asks me, "What are you reading?" The book is slipped between my knees but not hidden enough.

"*The Great Gatsby*. For English."

Jack laughs. "Wow, look at that, Barry. Your cousin's doing homework—on a Friday. Maybe you should try to be more like her." Barry always gets A's and B's, and I'm certain schoolbooks and assignments are the last thing he worries about on Friday afternoons.

He punches Jack in the arm but keeps talking to me. "What are you and Betsi going to do?"

"Pick up my birthday cake. My friends are coming over in a few hours," I say, tucking the book back into my bag.

"That's right. It's your birthday this weekend."

"Wait—girls are coming over?" Jack says. I don't think he can stand it unless everyone is paying attention to him in every situation. "Sounds like a sleepover to me!" He claps his hands together, like he just got a brilliant idea, and whistles.

"I don't believe you're invited," Barry tells him. "When's the family party again?" he asks me.

"Sunday. It's at your house, remember?" I say, trying to ignore Jack, who is staring at me.

"Right," Barry says, and then, "Well, okay, I guess I'll see you Sunday. Is Betsi coming soon?"

"I guess," I say, and just then she pulls up in her Jeep, the radio blasting an Elvis song. *We're caught in a trap . . . I can't walk out . . . Because I love you too much, baby.* She waves to us, and I turn around in time to see Barry give her the "call me" signal. I wonder if they are planning a surprise for me.

"Come on, Moran. We gonna leave sometime this year?" Jack says, less sarcastic and more like he's actually getting irritated.

"Yeah, yeah, settle down," Barry tells him, pushing Jack toward his truck. "Happy birthday," he adds before he walks away.

I grab my bag and run toward Betsi's Jeep. We have only a couple of hours left to pick up the cake and decorate the basement before the girls come over. Betsi volunteered to act as the official chaperone, and earlier this week we went to Kmart to buy decorations. Everything was mostly for fall or Halloween, but we found some with a tropical motif left over from the summer and on sale. Betsi decided we should keep with the theme and order Hawaiian pizza with pineapple and Canadian bacon and make a punch with Sprite and orange juice. We even found miniature grass skirts for the plastic tumblers. A Hawaiian cake sounded gross, so Mom special-ordered a chocolate cake with vanilla frosting and macadamia nuts. It's a rectangular cake, one layer, with a girl in a yellow-and-green-frosted hula skirt on the front and "Happy Birthday Presley" scrawled across the top in bright pink. Peter is spending tonight at Grandma Biddie's just to give us extra privacy. Everything is in place for the perfect party.

Betsi says, "Hey, birthday girl!" and gives me a big hug. Then she says, "I am so excited for your party. It's going to be great." She peels out of the parking lot, and I wish there were more people around to see me leaving in Betsi's open-top Jeep.

We head toward the bakery, and I pull my hair into a ponytail so it won't whip around from the wind. Betsi's hair has grown a little bit, and she has two rhinestone bobby pins holding her bangs back over her sunglasses, which are shaped like cat's eyes. "What was Barry doing?" she asks, turning the radio down and reaching for the cigarette lighter.

"Nothing. Just asking about the family party on Sunday. He didn't even remember it was at his house!" I tell her, watching her light the cigarette.

Betsi laughs the first drag out. "Figures!"

"He asked me if you were coming too."

"He did, huh?" she says, taking another drag and a left toward Magdalena's bakery. "Who was that other guy?"

"His best friend, Jack. He's annoying."

"Why? He's totally cute, and he was way into you."

"He was not!" I say, truly disgusted by the idea. "What makes you think that? You only saw him for, like, two seconds."

"Oh, believe me, I can tell," she says, mysterious and certain.

"Well, I totally hate him. He makes me feel stupid, and besides, he's a senior." I flip the radio stations for something current. "I did, however, make sure Chris Carroll knew I was having a party tonight."

"How can you even stand guys your own age?" she asks, pulling up in front of the bakery. "You're fourteen now. You need to broaden your horizons! Let me tell you something about love, Presley. There are some guys out there who are the kind of guys you want to spend a lifetime with, and there are others who are just more of a temporary comfort—like mashed potatoes and gravy. There's nothing wrong with mashed potatoes and gravy. In fact, it's important, sometimes even better, to go with the mashed potatoes and gravy, just as long as you don't get caught up in eating them for the rest of your life. Does that make sense?"

"Yes." I have no idea what she means.

"Did you know when I was a Crescent City Cavalier, I made out with the assistant coach for the boys' hockey team?"

"You did not!" I say.

"Yes, I did." She turns off the ignition. The sunlight catches the top of her mirrored glasses, bouncing off sideways and diagonal. "Tommy Shorer. He was twenty-two and just out of the state college. I used to go to the games. Everyone thought I was dating one of the defensemen, but really I'd wait for Tommy afterward, and he'd drive me home in his Chevy Nova and we'd turn off by St. Mary's and make out in the church parking lot. The next fall he moved to Boston to get his MBA, so that was that. But he was beautiful, and he was a man. And he was mashed potatoes and gravy." Betsi takes off her glasses so I can see her clearly in the light. "Aloha. Now let's go get that cake."

* * * * *

The basement is decorated with green and yellow and orange streamers, bright tropical colors to bring festive feelings into the room. Dad's card table is set up and covered by a paper tablecloth printed with palm trees around the edges. On top sit the pizza boxes, one plain cheese, the other with ham and pineapple, next to bowls of tortilla chips and salsa and candy dishes full of peanut M&M's, my favorite. The napkins and paper plates match the tablecloth, and we also bought leis in a different color for each girl—pink, yellow, red, and orange.

Betsi took some of her scarves and laid them over the lamps, so the light is hazy and warm like it is in dreams or when you first wake up and don't realize where you are.

Hannah is the first to arrive, with a large box wrapped perfectly in silver paper and an icy-blue bow. She brings it downstairs with her sleeping bag, also silver, the professional kind used for camping expeditions on places like Mount Everest. "My dad's," she explains, and I nod but pull one of the extra sheets Mom brought downstairs over my Crayola sleeping bag that I got in sixth grade. Luckily, Jill shows up moments later. Her bag is covered with rainbows and a giant unicorn in the center, and she makes no apologies for it. Her present is still in the Perry's drugstore sack, the envelope for the card unsealed. Karen shows up last, with a simple navy blue sleeping bag and a small box wrapped in Christmas paper. "It was all we had," she explains, shrugging and grabbing a handful of M&M's.

We turn up our favorite station on the radio—I already warned Betsi no Elvis records at this party—and pass around plates of pizza, licking the grease off our fingers as Betsi tells us stories about teachers she had at Cavalier High who are still there. "You guys have heard the rumors about Mrs. Franken and the Spanish teacher, right?"

"No way," says Jill. "I heard he was gay."

"Nah, he's just a little fem," Betsi assures us. "They are definitely getting it on. My ex–best friend Katie caught them after school one day when she went in for extra credit." The girls squeal with disgust at the image.

"Why don't you ever talk about Katie anymore?" I ask. When I was very young, they used to babysit me together. I have faint memories of Katie feeding me cheddar Goldfish crackers while Betsi stretched the kitchen phone as far as it would go to reach the back porch door so she could talk and smoke at the same time.

"Ugh." Betsi groans. "Don't remind me. What an evil bitch she turned out to be."

"What do you mean?" Karen asks.

"Oh, I was going out with this guy. Shit, what was his name? Brett. No, Brad. No, wait—it was Brent. Whatever. Anyway, Brent was always studying, and he never wanted to go out, so I broke up with him. Then, like two weeks later, Katie went on a date with him."

"But didn't you break up with him?" I ask.

"Well, technically—but Presley, that's not the point. There are certain codes of conduct between girlfriends that should be respected. Honestly, being friends with girls is so . . . draining. Girls are so competitive and backstabbing." We look around the room at one another and then at Betsi as she pulls pieces of pineapple off her slice of pizza, popping them in her mouth. When she realizes we're staring at her, she adds, "Oh, well, not you girls—you're different, I'm sure."

We're all too stuffed from pizza to move on to cake. Hannah says, "Why don't we call Chris Carroll?" in a singsongy voice.

I'm about to protest when Betsi says, "Screw the telephone. You don't need to call Chris Carroll to find out what he thinks. Your best bet for information is a Ouija board."

"Those are so fake," Karen says.

"Not if you use it right," Betsi says. She stands up and heads toward the toy closet where we keep the board games, Sorry, Trouble, Monopoly. She digs around in the back for a minute and pulls out a box.

"I didn't even know we had that," I say.

"It used to be mine. I gave it to your mom a long time ago

for you and Peter, but I can see that didn't happen. The trick is to balance the board on everyone's knees, not on the floor, so we have to sit real close, cross-legged, like this." Betsi has turned off all the lights and grabbed Dad's flashlight from his toolbox in the laundry room. She seems so certain that we follow her instructions without question, creating a pentagon. The letters face Betsi, and she places the pointer on the lower part of the board, what she calls the "neutral position," and tells each of us to place two fingers on the edge of it. Our hands all look different: Hannah's nails short and polished pearly pink; Jill's chewed and frayed and naked; Karen's manicured but clear; mine with chipped purple polish; and Betsi's long, red, and sharp, clicking on the plastic pointer.

"Now, we need to contact someone who has passed, who can act as our guide. How about Elvis?" We all groan. For a minute I wonder if maybe we should try to contact Aunt Marie, mostly to ask her if Dad will ever again acknowledge Betsi's presence. But no one else mentions Aunt Marie, not Betsi, not even Hannah who knew me back then, so I agree to Elvis and scoot in closer.

Dad's flashlight sits upright in the center, glowing and beaming toward the ceiling like a spotlight. Betsi tells us to close our eyes as she says in a low, serious, throaty voice, "Oh, Great Spirit World. We ask for the spirit of Elvis to come forth and guide us in our journey." Someone giggles—I think it's Jill, but Betsi shushes her and tries again. "Oh, Great Spirit of Elvis. Are you here to guide us through our journey?" It's completely silent except for the ticking of the furnace in the laundry room. On my back I think I feel the slightest chill, as if someone left a window open in another room, and then I feel the pointer move. We all open our eyes and see it turned toward the "Yes" printed on the board. No one asks who moved it, afraid to find out that maybe no one did.

Then Betsi says, "Thank you, Great Spirit of Elvis. Tell us . . . does someone in this room have a secret admirer?" The pointer circles around "Yes" again. I know I'm not moving it—at least I don't think I am—and everyone else seems fixated on the board. "Will the secret admirer reveal themselves soon?" she says, and the pointer begins to circle again but lingers in the corner. Betsi takes a deep breath and asks, "Great Spirit of Elvis. Can you tell us the name of the secret admirer?"

The pointer sits still for a moment and then begins creeping closer to the individual letters at the top of the board, circling around the beginning of the alphabet. I think it's about to spell it out for us, but then it slides abruptly back to "No" just as Mom opens the door at the top of the stairs and yells, "What are you guys doing down there?" We all shriek and the board flies up from our legs, the pointer rolling underneath the table.

"We're just playing a game," Betsi says, motioning toward us with her finger over her lips.

"Well, finish it up. It's time for cake." We scramble to put the board back in the box but have forgotten to pack the pointer when Mom and Dad come downstairs. Everyone begins to sing loud and off-key or in falsetto. Dad is carrying the cake with fourteen candles lit on top, the flames flickering over the hula girl so she looks almost alive. Our faces glow, and I watch Betsi catch Dad's eye. He continues singing but smiles at her for the first time in weeks. When I close my eyes and blow out the candles, I wish for everything to stay exactly how it is in this moment—no yelling, no whispers behind closed doors at night, no Betsi crying in her sleep, just everyone singing and waiting for their piece of something sweet.

* * * * *

We're all huddled in our sleeping bags with the lights off, watching *Grease* on the VCR for the third time that night. Betsi is in her makeshift sleeping bag of comforters and afghans on the floor next to me at the end of the row of girls. The opened gifts sit near the wall in a pile of paper and tissue—the LeSportsac purse Hannah brought, a stack of lip glosses and eye shadows from Jill, and a bracelet from Karen with charms of hearts and stars. Betsi's present will come tomorrow, at the family party.

We've all made bets on who will stay up the latest, but everyone is already asleep except for me and Betsi. We sing quietly under our breath, "Summer Nights" and "Look at Me, I'm Sandra Dee," but by "Hopelessly Devoted to You," I feel myself drifting off. I can sense light even behind my closed eyes, and I create my own movie. Chris Carroll knocks lightly on the basement window and brings me a small box with a silver locket on a chain. He presses it into my hand and kisses me softly on the lips, escaping back into the night, the locket warm in my palm like a secret.

I wake up before I find out what's inside. The TV screen glows bright blue, the VCR clock reads 1:58 A.M., and Betsi is gone. I sit up slightly, listening for sounds from upstairs, but there's nothing, just the ticking furnace again. I hear a small muffled noise, and then another, and I think it's Betsi on the phone in the laundry room. I creep toward the door, avoiding the spots in the carpet that have a tendency to creak, and get close enough to hear her say, "I think I'm in love with you." Then I walk backward, retracing my steps, and slide back beneath the crayons on my covers, wondering who is on the other end of the line before I fall back into sleep.

* * * * *

After a quick breakfast of hot apple cider and cinnamon toast, the girls gather their things, delivering their polite thank-yous to my parents as they leave. I am tasked with basement cleanup duty, and Betsi offers to help. In the daylight, the dust in the basement is more visible, coating the shelves near the TV and the lamp shades. Betsi attacks the rings left behind by our cups on the end tables with a bottle of Windex. I tug at the streamers taped to the corners of the ceiling, and some of them break in half. I crumple what I can in my hands, leaving behind some strands of color until I can get to a higher point.

I finally ask the question that has been running through my mind all morning: "Who were you on the phone with last night?"

Betsi stops humming "You're the One That I Want" and turns to face me, Windex still in hand. "What are you talking about?" she asks, her voice tight.

"I heard you. On the phone. Late last night?" She tries to keep her expression blank. "Do you have a boyfriend?" I drag out the last word, imitating Hannah's singsongy voice from last night, and continue with "Betsi's got a boyfriend, Betsi's got a boyfriend!"

"Oh, shut it, Pres. What are you, four or fourteen?" She sounds irritated, but just slightly, and she's also smirking. I take this as a sign that it's okay to continue my line of questioning.

"I won't say *anything*—I promise." I tie the garbage bag shut and flop down on the couch, hoping she'll join me. She does.

"Don't, because your mother will flip out and start asking questions, and I don't want to make a big deal out of it. God, I need a cigarette."

"It sounded like a big deal," I tell her, grabbing a stale left-over chip from the bowl on the table.

She laughs. "How much did you hear, you little shit?"

"Not that much." I pass her the bowl. "Enough," I admit. "What's he like?"

Betsi stops before taking a bite and thinks about her answer. "When he's with me, he acts completely different than he does when he's around everyone else. He's really sweet and open, and we laugh all the time. He says I make him laugh more than anyone has in years. He tells me I am the only person he doesn't have to pretend in front of. He says I make him feel alive."

"Oh." My mind is blank, my mouth empty of real words. I've never heard her talk like this. After a moment, I ask, "Do you love him?" Before I can stop myself, I add, "I heard you say you thought you did."

She snaps a quick look at me but waves away her initial response with her hand. "I don't know how I feel. It's complicated, Presley."

"How? Is he . . . mashed potatoes and gravy?"

Betsi is silent. When I look at her, I see her eyes watering, her lower lip quivering slightly. "He's—"

"How are you girls coming along down there?" Mom yells from the top of the stairs.

"We're almost finished," I yell back, shuffling the garbage bag for sound effect.

Betsi stands up quickly. "That's right, Pres. Just mashed potatoes and gravy. Our secret, okay?" she says, tucking the Windex underneath her arm and grabbing up her damp paper towels from around the room. I nod even though she isn't looking at me, fixated instead on a cobweb hovering near the last cluster of streamers that need to come down.

* * * * *

My party at Uncle Tim and Barry's house starts at 4:00 on Sunday, after church services and, more important, after the football game. Dad leaves for Uncle Tim's at noon to pick up a cake from the grocery store, which will likely be one of the generic ones from the bakery section, round and yellow with chocolate frosting. Maybe Dad will remember to ask them to add my name to the top. Mom says we should also take the left-over corner from my sleepover party cake. I pull the saran-wrapped chunk out of our freezer to defrost, staring at what's left: a portion of the Hawaiian girl's raised arm and her face, and the flowers around her neck cut off just above her bikini.

"I'll stay at Tim's until you get there," Dad tells my mother. "No sense in coming back this way." Uncle Tim and Barry live only five minutes away from us by car, and sometimes we even walk over there if the weather is good enough and we're not carrying too much. We both know what Dad really wants to do—park himself on the couch with Uncle Tim to watch the Lions play at 1:00.

"They're brothers," Mom explains as Dad backs out of the driveway. "That's what brothers do."

As expected, when the rest of us get there, we find Dad and Uncle Tim planted in front of the TV with their feet on the coffee table, chips and beef jerky spread out next to a few cans of beer, arguing about who made the better play and why the team was robbed once again. Mom hands me a large tray of her homemade lasagna to take to the kitchen and goes back outside for the rest of the foil-covered items. Betsi carries in a bowl of what she calls her specialty, a salad with Italian dressing and homemade croutons and freshly shredded Parmesan cheese. The rule is, whoever hosts the party doesn't have to supply the food or cook, just get the place clean and tidy up afterward. I'd rather be in charge of the food, because whenever we host the parties, I'm always the one who gets stuck dusting, loading the dishwasher, and throwing things away.

I like it best when we go to Uncle Tim's for parties; his house always feels the most comfortable and warm. Mom and Dad have been trying to talk him into moving into one of the smaller flats on the south side of town for years, but his answer is always the same: "It's just too much trouble to move. I'll wait until after Barry graduates." Everything in the house is just as it was when Aunt Marie was alive—the family photos still hanging on the wall, the living room windows draped with cornflower-blue curtains she sewed herself, and the outside trim still the same sage green she painted to match her garden. I see pieces of her in all corners every time I come over, and I think it's the real reason Uncle Tim wants to stay, but I keep this to myself.

The group today is small—Aunt Helen and her family are at my cousin John's soccer tournament, three hours away in Kalamazoo, but she dropped off a card before they left. That's fine by me, because they always give me money whether they're at the party or not, usually twenty or sometimes even thirty dollars. I'm not sure what I'm getting from everyone else. I saw Betsi bring in another bag from the trunk, and even though she had her jacket thrown over it, I could tell it was my presents. I asked Mom and Dad for a telephone for my room, one of those see-through plastic ones that come in colors like hot pink and light up when they ring. Mom didn't seem too excited about that idea. Betsi has been jumpy and secretive about her present for me, taunting me with "I have something for you" and "I know something you don't know." I keep wandering by the pile on Uncle Tim's dining room table and see a box marked TO PRESLEY, FROM BARRY, and wonder if it's something Barry actually picked out himself.

All of the coats are taken up to Barry's room and piled on the bed. In my coat pocket, I carry one of the lipsticks I got from Jill, Starlight Express, a sheer pink with a touch of glitter. Mom doesn't say anything when she sees it on my lips, probably because it's my birthday, but Grandma Dunn asks, "What's that on your mouth?" She and Grandpa won't head back down to Florida until after the first of the year, with the other snowbirds.

"It's lip gloss, Grandma," Betsi says. "Here, why don't you let me fix you up a plate of food?" She steers Grandma Dunn into the living room. I throw Betsi a "thanks" as she passes by. I'm listening to Uncle Tim's small radio that sits on the kitchen windowsill. I cut up pieces of garlic bread fresh from the oven, placing them in a basket lined with cloth napkins to keep them warm. Barry sneaks up behind me, reaching over my shoulder for a carrot stick on the vegetable tray, his chest brushing against my back.

"How was your sleepover?" he asks.

"Fine. It wasn't really a sleepover," I try to explain.

"Oh. I thought your friends spent the night."

"Well, they did."

"So how is that *not* a sleepover?" Barry asks, laughing and this time reaching for a cauliflower stalk.

"Well, it is sort of, but not like a kid's sleepover—"

"Wait," he says, grabbing my shoulder suddenly. "Do you hear that?" He leans over the bread basket and turns up the volume on the radio. I recognize Elton John's voice but can't remember the title.

"This is *such* a great song," he says, closing his eyes and nodding in time with the music. I don't know what to say, so I start to ask Barry what the name of the song is, but he motions for me to be quiet. He shuffles around the kitchen, singing along with the music. "'Until you've seen this trash can dream come true . . . You stand at the edge while people run you through . . .'"

His voice is clear and rich. I didn't even know Barry could sing. He drops the cauliflower on the counter, grabbing my hands and trying to twirl me across the room. "'And I thank the Lord there's people out there like you . . . I thank the Lord there's people out there like you.'" I giggle with embarrassment as I let him spin me around and find Betsi watching us from the doorway, smiling just like the Mona Lisa that Elton John and Barry are singing about at the top of their lungs, as though their lives depended on it.

* * * * *

Mom hands me a paper bag with handles and tells me to pack up my gifts while she loads Uncle Tim's dishwasher. Really, it should be Uncle Tim doing the straightening, but he's asleep on one couch and Barry has wandered off. Dad snoozes on the other couch while Peter plays with Barry's game system, the sound effects turned down low. The grandparents are playing cards in the dining room. I transfer my pile into the bag: a baby-blue cardigan mailed from Grandma Biddie; a bright red hat and scarf from Grandma and Grandpa Dunn; a Cavaliers sweatshirt from Uncle Tim; and a new book bag from Peter, who made sure to point out that Mom chose it. Even though Mom and Dad ended up getting me the hot-pink phone I wanted—with a warning of "No calls until your homework is done."—I think it's Barry's and Betsi's gifts I like best.

I opened Barry's first, a book he disguised by wrapping it in a larger box. "I didn't want you to be able to tell what it was just by walking by," he said, winking.

"*Tender Is the Night,*" I said, announcing the title to the room and hoping the "ohs!" from the adults will buy me some time to figure out why he chose this particular one.

"*Gatsby* is a great story, but I thought you should check something out by Fitzgerald that wasn't assigned reading," Barry explained. "He really nails the complications of love. I read somewhere that he once said *Gatsby* was a tour de force but that this book was a real confession of faith."

The "ohs" fell silent upon Barry's impromptu dissertation. My mother spoke first. "Barry . . . I had no idea you were such a . . . *voracious* reader."

"Here," Betsi said to me, disregarding the bemused looks everyone was giving Barry. "Open mine next." Her present was in a dark purple gift bag with lavender tissue peeking out. I reached in and pulled out a box covered in red, orange, and green jewels, with little mirrors sewn into gold fabric. When I lifted the lid, there was the smallest tinkling of music. The inside of the box was lined with the same fabric around a mirror.

"Do you know what song it is?" Betsi asked. I held the box up to my ear like a seashell, but I still couldn't tell. She started to sing softly: "'Only fools . . . rush . . . in . . . But I . . . can't help . . . falling in love with you.'"

"It sounds so different than the version you play," I told her.

"I know. I wanted to try and find a way to make you see what I love, but in a different way. I wanted to give you something that was a little part of me. You can keep anything in there, bracelets, earrings, barrettes, notes, secrets. It's yours."

Now, packing up, I place the box in the paper bag last,

holding it in my hands with the lid open and staring at my reflection. The mirror is so small, I can see only my mouth. Most of the glitter has faded from my lips. I push myself up, heading for Barry's room to retrieve my new lipstick from my coat pocket.

Dusk is falling, and the leftover light coming in through the windows of the upstairs hallway creates long, willowy shadows of a lamp, a vase, me. I wonder if I should turn on a light, but I can still make out the door to Barry's room at the end of the hall, a ray coming through the crack at the bottom to guide me. When I turn the handle, the door sticks. I give it a good rattle, but it won't budge. "Hello?" I say, knocking lightly. "It's Presley. Can you open the door? I need my coat."

I hear a shifting on the other side, just slightly, like a hiccup. It's there and then it's gone. I lean my ear toward the door, trying to hold my breath, and then I hear it again, first a creaking and then a murmur, as if someone is turning in their sleep. Then I hear Betsi's voice say, "Coming!" and it seems like forever before the door opens. Her hair is sticking up in the back, and her eyes are squinting even though the light has been on in the room. The coats are piled on the bed but smashed down in the center. "I fell asleep," Betsi explains, shrugging.

"Up here? Why didn't you just go into another room without coats on the bed?" I ask her, heading over to the heap and pulling on the sleeve of my jacket, which is at the bottom. When I lift it up, something crumpled up and black falls onto the bed. I pick it up, unraveling it in my hand, and see it's a bra. "Is this yours?" I ask, holding it like a dead mouse.

"Oh, yeah. I must have slipped it off while I was sleeping. I do that sometimes—take off my clothes in my sleep. It's the craziest thing," Betsi says, laughing a little and grabbing the bra from my hands.

"Yeah. Crazy," I say, reaching into the pocket of my coat for my gloss.

Betsi takes off her shirt right in front of me to put her bra back on. She's standing near Barry's closet door, and before she refastens it, I can't help but notice her breasts, how perfectly round they are, how rosy the centers seem against her smooth skin, which is the color of fresh whipped cream. Betsi catches my eye in the mirror on the door and I look away, trying to find something else to concentrate on—the sports trophies on Barry's desk, a pair of tube socks on his chair, math papers on the floor.

"Have you seen Barry around?" I ask.

Betsi stares straight into the mirror, fixing the back of her hair and humming slightly. She says, "Nope. Haven't seen him. I was asleep, remember?" She turns around and winks at me. "You havin' a good birthday?" I nod. "Good. Let's go downstairs and get some more cake before Grandpa and Grandma leave with half of it, huh?" She places her hand on my shoulder to guide me, reaching back with the other to turn off the light as we walk through the doorway. The outside light is almost completely gone now, and the shadows in the hallway are beginning to fade and blend with the darkness. But when we get to the top of the stairs, I sense another shadow moving from the corner of my eye, dancing near Barry's room and then disappearing into the bathroom like a ghost. Halloween is just a month away, and I think about whether I'm too old to go out trick-or-treating anymore. I decide it might be fun to dress up and pretend to be something else for one more year.

Chapter 4

Trick or Treat

The hardest part about carving pumpkins is pulling out the guts. Only then can you really begin to cut into the shell. Betsi and I have spread out old issues of the *Times* across the kitchen floor to help contain the mess. Our hands are dusty with newsprint, but we grab our weapons, knives with plastic orange handles made especially for jack-o'-lantern use. Betsi has promised she'll be in charge of removing the insides; she is brave. I can't stand reaching in or how it feels in my hands, cold and stringy and endless.

This year we bought two medium-size pumpkins, one for each side of the front porch steps. Betsi is attempting a more complicated design, a black cat with an arched back, the kind that looks like it's screeching and spooked. I'm sticking to the traditional approach: triangle eyes and nose with a jagged, nearly toothless mouth. We cut around the stems, and after I lift off the top, I pass my pumpkin over to Betsi to take care of the dirty business. Mom, Dad, and Peter are out running errands.

"You going out for Devil's Night this year?" she asks, dumping pumpkin guts onto the newspaper and shaking her hands to get rid of the sticky seeds left behind. Chris Carroll asked me the same question earlier in the week during gym class. Around here the tradition breaks down to a lot of houses draped in toilet paper and iced with shaving cream. If you're someone like Fred Portis, who is always complaining at city council meetings about kids skateboarding near the library, it can also involve rotten eggs tossed at your windows. In middle school, I heard rumors about the high school kids raising the ante by making shit bombs: left-behind dog droppings stuffed inside a paper bag and smashed against a front door. I'm pretty sure Barry's been out several times in his high school career, and even launched a shit bomb or two, but not me—I've always been too scared of getting caught.

"No, I don't think so. What's the point?"

"What's the point? It's tradition! It's fun! Now that you're in high school, you have to go out at least once." I know what Betsi is going to say next, and my prediction comes true. "I went out *every* year of high school, and middle school too."

I am starting to realize that I am not living up to expectations. I'm less than two full months into school, but it's already becoming clear to me that our family, both sides, has a reputation of being recognized. Barry's advice was administered during the Fourth of July fireworks on the lake at the cottage. We sat on towels waiting for the light to fall away from the sky and the show to begin while the younger cousins ran around the beach holding lit sparklers.

"So what's the plan for the fall? You going out for any sports?" Barry asked. His tan was well established by then, his golden arms resting on top of his bent knees.

"I haven't really thought about it. I didn't exactly play a lot of sports in middle school." I was chewing on the plastic orange straw sticking out of my lemonade glass.

"That's not a big deal. You seem like you'd pick things up pretty quickly. No need to be perfect." He picked up a stick nearby and started tracing circles into the sand.

"But you are. At sports. Lots of things." I bit my lip to stop myself from gushing any further, but it was true. Barry made his mark in athletics and academics—he was involved in a sport every season, took college-prep history and English, and still managed to find time to edit the school paper.

Behind us, Aunt Helen yelled at her kids: "Stop running around with those sparklers before you fall and burn your eye out!" My cousins froze and began waving the sticks in rapid circles while standing in place.

"I'm just saying it might be smart to start thinking about ways to get involved. That's all college recruiters care about— how you look on paper. I'm sure it doesn't seem like it right now, but you'll be a senior before you know it." Barry stood up, brushing the sand off his board shorts. "Think it's too late to go swimming?"

"The fireworks are going to start soon. We're not supposed to go in the water after dark," I reminded him.

"Right," he said, and then sprinted into the water. None of the parents objected. I wasn't sure they had even noticed. I wondered if he wanted me to follow, but when I looked back, he had already drifted too far away from the shore for me to catch up.

". . . homecoming?" I hear only the last fragment of Betsi's question.

"What?"

"Are you going to homecoming?" she repeats.

"Oh. I don't think so." The homecoming game and dance are later this year, the weekend after Halloween. "Isn't it mostly juniors and seniors who go?"

"Well, yes, but that's not a rule or anything. You have a much better chance of going, because the upperclassmen like taking younger girls. I went *every* year," she says.

"Yes, I remember." Not only did she go every year, but she was crowned homecoming queen as a senior. After the fire in the den, she took out a bunch of old high school photos to help make the place feel "more familiar," propping them up in the windowsill next to the pull-out couch. Each dance photo showed her with a different date: senior boys when she was a freshman, freshman boys when she was a senior. By graduation she had also earned the titles of Best-Looking and Class Clown, as well as Most Likely to Become a Groupie.

"You need to take advantage of these moments, Pres. They're all that really matter. Grades, quizzes, exams? It's all just bullshit." Her words of wisdom are the complete opposite of Barry's, but I've seen all the evidence that supports her side of the argument: her yearbooks with the important pages bookmarked by dance ticket stubs, cigar boxes crammed with dead corsages and candid photos, wrinkled formal wear shoved into banker boxes, still stained with cigarette ash and alcohol. It's like the Betsi Museum, and I am the most frequent visitor.

"Chris Carroll and a bunch of people are going out," I tell Betsi as she scrapes the inner walls of my pumpkin.

"How do you know that?" Betsi asks.

"He told me."

"See, that's what I'm talking about. He told you because he wanted to see if you had any interest in going too."

"Oh, no . . . I don't think so."

Betsi stops midscrape. "Jesus, Presley. You have got a lot to learn about picking up signals from guys."

She has a point. Betsi's much more of an expert in this area, and she must be doing something right, because she goes out almost every night, though none of us are sure who with or if it's even the same person. Mom is always probing Betsi for more details, but Betsi keeps saying that she doesn't want to jinx it by revealing anything too soon. I'm pretty sure it's the same guy I heard her talking to on the phone the night of my birthday, but I haven't asked her about him since then. I just hope he doesn't drink. Betsi's been going to her meetings on a regular basis, and I haven't seen her with a glass of wine since the summer.

"Here you go!" Betsi hands over the hollow gourd, far lighter now and ready for carving. I take a sharpened pencil and sketch out my incision plans. If I don't create a blueprint first, I end up cutting the eyes either too close or one way bigger than the other.

"Are you going out tonight?" I try to make it sound like I don't care one way or another.

"Hmm. Not sure," Betsi says, finishing up her own pumpkin. "Probably." It's already getting dark outside, and the rest of the family will pull into the driveway before too long. I figure my only chance of getting her to tell me more about the mashed-potatoes-and-gravy guy is when we're alone, though my window of time is shrinking quickly.

"So is this like a meeting, or something else?" I stab my knife into the left eye of my soon-to-be jack-o'-lantern and hope for the best.

"Meeting?" Betsi seems genuinely confused.

"You know. Your group meetings."

"Oh. Right. Um, no, not tonight." She holds the black-cat pattern up to her pumpkin. It's a complicated procedure that involves pricking dozens and dozens of tiny pinholes into the surface before cutting everything away. It seems like a lot of effort, especially for something that might not even work out the way you want it to. I don't know why Betsi bothers.

"So is it a mashed-potatoes kind of night?" I think I've made the mouth too big and try to compensate for it on the other side of the toothy grin.

"Something like that. Hey. You should really think about going out with your friends on Devil's Night. There's nothing wrong with stirring up a little mischief." We look up from our pumpkins and lock eyes. Betsi's lips part just a bit, as if the words are trying to push their way through. Then there's the sound of the garage door lifting, and her lips seal shut again. She glances at the kitchen clock.

"Damn, I didn't realize it was so late. I need to jump in the shower. You don't mind if we finish this up tomorrow, do you?"

Before I can answer, she's darted up the stairs, and I hear the screech of the shower handles and the water warming up. Betsi's pumpkin is still sitting on the floor, empty and punctured. I set the interrupted piece of work over a clean sheet of newspaper on the windowsill so she won't forget to finish what she started.

★ ★ ★ ★ ★

Hannah and I are splitting a banana for lunch, based on some diet she read about in her mother's stack of magazines. I already know my chances of making it through the entire week on this plan are slim to none, but I play along. I'm trying to be a good sport so I can convince Hannah to come out on Devil's Night with Chris and his friends.

"I don't know, it sounds kind of lame," she says, chewing her half of the banana slowly, like the article suggests.

"I know, but I really like him, and he asked if both of us wanted to go. We can tell our parents we're babysitting. They won't even know we're gone," I tell her, somewhat surprised by my own idea. Halloween falls on a Friday this year, which means Devil's Night is Thursday, a school night. "I bet I could get Betsi to cover for us too, if we needed it."

"Presley, no offense, but sometimes I think your aunt Betsi is more like your crazy sister home from college."

"She's not crazy."

"I didn't mean crazy-crazy, I just meant a little . . . different. You know, from normal aunts." Hannah folds the banana peel as if she's trying to put it back together. "I'm not really worried about cover stories. My parents are both in trial right now, so I'm pretty sure I'd need to light myself on fire before they noticed anything out of the ordinary."

"So? Will you come?"

"Toilet paper and shaving cream, huh? Oh, what the hell. When you see Carroll in gym class at the end of the day, tell him we're in."

"Thank you, thank you, thank you!" I squeal, as if I've just won the Chris Carroll lottery.

"Jesus, don't make a scene." Hannah tosses the banana peel in the garbage can. "Wow. I can't believe how full I feel."

"Full. Right. Me too." I don't have the heart to tell her the banana diet is a bust. As we walk out of the cafeteria, Hannah fixates on something in the corner. "Hey. Isn't that your cousin?"

I look at where she's pointing, at a kid sitting by himself, slumped over the table like he's sleeping. "No, of course not—" I start to say, but then I see the varsity jacket draped over his chair and recognize the number on the back.

"Catch up with you later?" I say. Hannah nods, and I make my way over to Barry. His head is actually resting on a pile of textbooks with loose-leaf sheets crumpled and crammed in between the pages.

"Barry?"

His head jerks. "Pres. Hey. I didn't realize anyone was there."

I slip into the chair across from him. Barry's shirt is on inside out, and I don't think his hair has seen a brush or a shower in several days. His eyes are sinking into black rings, and he's surrounded by an open bag of corn chips and three empty Coke cans. Maybe he should've had four.

"You okay?" I ask, even though I can see he's not.

"Me? Oh, sure. Just a little catnap before afternoon classes. I haven't been getting much sleep lately. You know how the homework piles up." Barry runs his fingers through his hair and attempts a smile. "How are you? Anyone giving you a hard time?" He motions like he'll punch anyone who might fit the bill.

"No, not really. It's not as bad as I thought it would be. I kinda think you get more of a break when you're a girl, you know?"

"You're a fast learner, Presley. By the way, that rule doesn't change once you leave high school." Barry glances at his watch. "Damn. I was supposed to meet Jack twenty minutes ago. You didn't happen to see him come through here, did you?"

"No, I don't think so."

"What's that about?" Barry asks, cocking his head to the left and smirking.

"What?" I ask, wiping my nose just in case.

"You rolled your eyes when I asked about Jack."

"I did? I didn't mean to."

"He's actually a really good guy. I know he acts like a smart-ass in front of you, but he's solid." Barry shuffles his empty Coke cans into a clustered triangle. "You know, he was the only one of my friends to show up at my mom's funeral."

"Really? I sort of remember him being there, but I didn't know he was the only one."

"Yeah. He probably knows more about me than anyone— almost anyone." Barry leans closer and lowers his voice. "So I heard you might be going out this week for Devil's Night?"

"Who told you that?" My cheeks feel hot, like Barry just caught me lip-synching to my mirror.

"Betsi."

"When did you see Betsi?"

"She came by to pick up something from my dad," Barry mumbles, standing up. He tucks his mess of books and papers underneath one arm, walks around toward me, and places his other hand on my shoulder. "Don't worry, Pres. I won't tell anyone."

"Moran!" The voice is easily recognizable, but one I don't usually hear until the end of the day. We both turn to see Mr. Lyndon standing behind us, arms folded, rocking back and forth slowly on the heels of his stark white athletic shoes.

"What? I mean, yes?" I stammer, convinced he's figured out that I don't really run the full ten laps to warm up in class.

"Not you. You," he says, pointing to the other Moran, Barry, who apparently is on trial for assassinating the president. "You want to explain to me why you've missed the last three practices? You want to tell me why I shouldn't bench you for Saturday's game? The rest of the season?"

If Barry was catnapping five minutes ago, he's wide awake now, his eyes darting between me and the enraged coach. "I can explain," he pleads. "Just give me a second."

The bell is ringing in the background, signaling the end of the lunch period and, quite possibly, the beginning of several rounds between Lyndon and Barry. This is clearly not an exchange I'm meant to witness or know about. This time I am the one who puts my hand on Barry's shoulder and leans close.

"Don't worry. I won't tell anyone," I whisper, because we're family, and keeping secrets seems to be what we do best.

* * * * *

"Remind me again," Hannah asks, "why we fabricated a babysitting story to sneak out with Chris Carroll and his two Zombies to papier-mâché the neighborhood. What is so great about him, anyway?"

I am starting to ask myself the same question. Hannah and I are on our way to the corner of Wilson and Kensington, chosen because Chris said the old brick bus shelter on the corner offered a good rendezvous point.

"I mean, really, Pres," Hannah goes on. "You've had, like, what—five conversations with him? He's not even that cute." She is right about the first part; most of my exchanges with

Chris have been during gym class, in less than desirable condi-
tions. I've never been an athletic superstar like Barry, but I can
usually hold a solid B in gym class. This year is becoming a
catalog of pratfalls, with Chris bearing witness: first with basketball, a series of missed layups and overthrown foul shots,
and now with soccer, where I miss foot-to-ball contact on a
regular basis. Last week Mr. Lyndon pulled me aside after class
to ask if I'd had my eyes examined recently. What I wanted to
say was "No, it's not that I can't see the ball—it's that I can see
Chris Carroll watching me," but I nodded and said I'd look
into it.

"I don't know, I just like him. I think he's cute and funny.
And he asked if we wanted to hang out with him, so that must
mean something, right?" I say.

"I hope so. I'm missing at least three omelets for this guy,"
she says. Hannah and I were in charge of procuring the eggs. At
this time of year, eggs are one shopping-list item that sets off
alarms in the neighborhood grocery stores, especially when
they're being purchased by teenagers and not adults. We
decided to cobble together what we could from our own refrig-
erators, splitting the ransacked quantity evenly between house-
holds so as to remain unnoticed. We left behind the original
carton and wrapped the eggs in kneesocks, placing them in a
Tupperware container tucked discreetly into my backpack.

Daylight savings time kicked in last week, and with the
hands of the clock moved back an hour, we are blessed with
darkness falling earlier in the night to help cloak our actions. On
the way over with our smuggled eggs, we shuffle through piles
of fallen leaves, trying to remain casual every time a pair of
headlights comes into view. Pumpkins flicker from the porches
of most houses, and some neighbors have lined up fake tomb-

stones in their front lawns. There are even a few bloody corpses made from old clothes stuffed with newspapers, lying on the ground as if they've resurrected and tried to crawl from their own graves to tell us what really happened.

Chris Carroll is already waiting inside the bus stop with his two sidekicks—the Zombies, Jeff and Jayar. I have a hard time telling the two apart, especially when they're wearing baseball hats, like they are tonight. Chris is smoking, and I try not to act surprised.

"You guys bring the eggs?" Chris asks, taking short, quick puffs.

"Of course we did," says Hannah. "That's not a cigar, you know. Do you even really smoke?" She's standing close enough to me so I can jam my elbow into her ribs without it being visually obvious, but her loud, yelping "What?" doesn't help keep my cover.

I'm waiting for Chris to laugh, to tell us how lame we are or that our services are no longer required, but he just nods slowly, throwing the cigarette on the ground and smashing the embers underneath his Adidas.

"You're right. I don't really smoke. Sorry about that."

I'm starting to think maybe Mr. Lyndon is right and that I should have my eyes checked after all.

The boys make a pile of weapons in the center of the bus stop: twelve rolls of toilet paper, two and a half cans of menthol shaving cream, and the eggs, still intact in their sock incubators.

"That's all we've got?" Hannah asks, rearranging her scarf for the fourth time since we got here. I'm going to owe her big for this one.

"We decided to hit one target, hard, instead of several small ones. Makes a bigger impact," Sergeant Chris explains.

"Cool," I tell him, even though he clearly wasn't talking to me. "Good idea." Hannah snorts, while the Zombies grunt and distribute the ammunition evenly among our backpacks. "So who's the target?" I ask.

"Lyndon," Chris says, and the Zombies high-five each other, though I'm not sure why.

"Lyndon? Do you know if he's home?" Hannah asks.

"Maybe. We'll have to be quick. And quiet. The eggs will probably draw the most attention, so we'll do those last." Chris is obviously taking this very seriously. "I made a map so we all know our positions." He pulls out a piece of graph paper from his back pocket, the kind we use in math class.

"How did you figure out where he lives?" I ask.

"Hey, Pres, it's not like teachers are in the Witness Protection Program," Chris says. The Zombies snort, and even Hannah giggles.

"Right," I say, hoping no one can see the flush filling my cheeks. Chris motions for everyone to come closer and review the map. All the key points around Lyndon's house are marked with thick, black X's. On the east side, near the driveway, two X's for the Zombies. On the rear west corner, behind the house, two X's—for Chris and Hannah. The final X is in the front of the house, behind what I assume is a large oak tree.

"Shouldn't someone be out front with me?" I ask.

"That's the most visible and important position, so we don't want more than one person out front or it might draw attention," Chris explains, refolding the map and sliding it into his back pocket. "Plus, there's really only room for one to take cover behind the tree."

"I'll take the front position," Hannah says, trying to throw me a lifesaver.

"No!" Chris yells a little too loudly. He lowers his voice. "I mean, I need your arm, Hannah. We're in charge of the eggs, and, well, you throw a lot better than Pres does. No offense."

I make an immediate mental flip to one of the Ten Commandments of Presley—*Make fun of thyself first*—and wave Chris off with a talk-show-host laugh. "Oh, hell, I'd probably end up hitting myself in the head by accident."

We file out of the bus stop, and the Zombies take the lead, making the "ch-ch-ch-ah-ah-ah" sound from the *Friday the 13th* movies. Chris follows, and Hannah falls back to talk to me while I bring up the rear.

"Let's just go," she says through her teeth.

"No way! Lyndon deserves this," I say a little too merrily. "He really chewed out Barry the other day."

"What for?"

"Just football-practice stuff, but he was such a dick about it. You'd better catch up with Chris, we'll need to break off in a few blocks."

"You sure you're okay?" Hannah asks.

"Of course. Now go!" I maintain my smile until Hannah's safely in front of me, and then I erase it like chalk on a board, shoving my hands into my coat pockets for warmth. For the next few blocks, I catch myself playing that old game of trying to avoid the sidewalk cracks among the wet leaves while chanting in my head, *It's not her fault, it's not her fault,* over and over. Above me, constellations peek from the clear October sky— Orion, the Big Dipper, Cassiopeia. Betsi was the person who taught me how to trace the stars, and they come into focus much more quickly now.

Lyndon's block is abandoned and still. The houses here sit closer together, and the decorations are sparse. Older people live in this part of town, their grown kids long since moved away. On Halloween night, most of the porch lights will remain dark, the front doors shut, signaling a refusal to participate in a holiday geared toward children and candy.

The Zombies take their position behind the minivan parked in the driveway, toilet paper in one hand and shaving cream in the other. Chris and Hannah move back behind the bushes on the other side of the house. There aren't any porch lights on, but there's a dim glow peeking through the large window on the first floor.

The plan is this: as soon as we hear the eggs hit the house, everyone is to retreat to the bus stop to reconvene. One long whistle is the all-clear to begin the damage, while three short whistles are the signal to abort. I am the gatekeeper. I peek around the tree one more time; the glow from the downstairs window is brighter now, the curtain open. I can see Lyndon sitting in the room, the light from the TV bouncing off the walls. It looks like he's shoveling bites into his mouth from a plate held in his hands. I'm fairly certain he's still wearing his gym-teacher outfit. He's seated near the window, as if he knows his time has come, but he won't go down without a fight—and a full stomach.

I think about what Betsi said: "There's nothing wrong with stirring up a little mischief." And as I walk directly ahead of the tree to keep myself out of the line of sight, I choose my signal— one long whistle—leaving behind the scene of the crime as the shrill tweet escapes from my lips. It is exactly ten blocks east and two blocks south to my house, and I don't need Chris Carroll to make me a map to tell me how to get home.

* * * * *

By the time I get to my street, clouds have draped themselves across the night sky, and the constellations have disappeared. I button my coat all the way to the top and wonder, if Chris or Hannah or the Zombies got caught, whether they would implicate me to Lyndon, whether I even cared.

Instead of two carved pumpkins on each side of our house stoop, there's just one—mine—and the candle struggles to flicker inside. The opposite side of the porch is occupied by Betsi, whose lit cigarette burns almost brighter than the jack-o'-lantern.

"How'd it go?" she asks. Her voice seems cold and flat.

"It was stupid. I left."

She nods and continues to smoke.

"Where's your pumpkin?" I demand, my words unusually clipped.

"It's not officially Halloween yet. I still have time to make everything the way we wanted it to be."

"Do you?" I snap.

Betsi takes another drag from her cigarette, blowing the smoke directly toward me. For the first time, I notice a red plastic cup at her feet.

"What's that?"

"Hey, Pres, get off my back. You're not the Betsi police. You're just a kid, and you don't know what it's like to try and survive in my world."

"Actually, Betsi, I think we're all trying to survive in your world." It might be the first honest thing that's come out of my mouth all night, but Betsi just lights up another cigarette and doesn't say a word. My body shudders, maybe from the chill in the air, or maybe the silence between us. We are staring at each other, but she doesn't see me. She has dark glass marbles for eyes.

Then she picks up her red cup and swallows long and hard.

I walk up our stoop, stopping midway to lean down and lift the lid off my pumpkin, blowing out what little light is left.

* * * * *

That night I dream about my school cafeteria. It's snowing outside, but the windows have been wedged open, and the wind blows the napkins and food wrappers from the trays. The cafeteria is full of students, but no one talks. I see Hannah sitting at a table stacked with bananas ripe for peeling, and I try to catch her eye. She ignores me, rearranging the fruit into a pyramid. Chris Carroll is standing in the hot-food line smoking a cigarette, and no one objects. I decide to look for Barry and head toward the corners of the cafeteria, thinking I might find him curled up on top of his textbooks. The only trace left behind is his jacket, draped over the chair to mark his place. He is nowhere to be found.

"It's time to go."

The announcement comes over the PA system. Everyone around me stands up and I try to grab some of the people passing me by to ask where we're all going. No one will answer. I don't recognize any of the students except Hannah and Chris, and they don't see me. Nobody can see me. Then the cafeteria is empty except for me and Barry's jacket. I wait for him as the PA announcement repeats over and over again: "It's time to go. It's time to go."

* * * * *

The next morning is Halloween, and when I wake up, I am still in my clothes from the night before, my sheets twisted and wrapped like ropes around my legs. My hair is plastered over my forehead in hot wisps. When I try to sit up, the room spins and blurs. I'm on a carnival ride, the one that's shaped like a cylinder that spins and sucks you to the wall before the floor drops out from underneath.

"Mom!" I yell for her just like I did when I was younger, but this time she doesn't run into my room within seconds of my distress call. My clock radio reads 7:12, and a light rain taps against the windows. "Mom!" I try again with a longer though not louder wail—I've reached my maximum volume.

I hear her familiar footsteps coming up the stairs, and then she appears in my doorway, wiping her hands with a dish towel, her hair tied back in a bun. She takes one look at me and says, "Let me get the thermometer." For once I know I'm not going to need my bed lamp to help my cause.

I hold the thermometer steady under my tongue until my mother takes it from me. "A hundred and one. Okay, kiddo, I'll go call the school. Jesus, between the two of you, I should open an infirmary."

"What do you mean?"

"Betsi's sick too. Head cold. But she's far more mobile than you are. You should give Hannah a call and ask her to pick up your assignments so you don't get behind. You can catch up this weekend if you start feeling better. Ask her to drop your books and things on the way home from school today."

"Hannah. Right." I stare at the pink phone next to my bed.

"Something wrong, Presley?"

"No. No, I'm just hot. And dizzy. Can I have some juice?"

"Of course. I'll be right back."

The numbers on my phone seem to stare at me with disapproval. I lift the handset, and my finger hovers above the first digit of Hannah's number.

"You got yourself into this," my phone says, taunting me. "Now you need to get yourself out of it."

"Oh, shut up," I mutter, and finish dialing. Hannah answers on the second ring.

"Hey, it's me," I say.

"Oh, hey. You sound terrible!" She sounds like she's chewing on toast. I guess she's decided to temporarily ditch the bananas.

"Yeah, I'm sick. I have a fever and everything," I tell her, as if I'm trying to convince her.

"But it's Halloween! You'll miss all the little kids dressed up." The first-, second-, and third-graders from the elementary school two blocks over walk in buddy pairs to our school, where the gym is transformed by the senior class into a kid-friendly haunted house with stations set up for trick-or-treating. The best part is watching the children parade through the neighborhood in their costumes—a two-and-a-half-foot-tall horde of face-painted goblins, fairy princesses crowned with tiaras, and plastic-smocked Teenage Mutant Ninja Turtles.

"Take pictures for me?" I ask.

"Of course," she says. We've been talking for over a minute now, and Hannah has yet to unleash a fury on me for ditching last night. "So you got home okay last night?"

"Um, yeah . . . Wait, aren't you mad?"

"Mad about what? Didn't Betsi tell you I called?"

"No!"

"Yeah, I ditched as soon as you gave the signal. I figured it was better to just head home than back to the stupid bus shelter."

"Right," I say, remembering my one long whistle. Did I get my signals crossed?

"Those guys are idiots. I can't believe they stayed behind. I hope they got busted."

Guess it wasn't me who got my signals mixed up. I mouth a silent thank-you and count my blessings that Hannah's memory isn't always the sharpest part of her personality.

"So, you're not mad, are you?" Hannah asks.

"Me? No! Why would I be mad?"

"Oh, you know, the whole Chris thing. He really is a jack-ass."

"Totally! I don't know what I was thinking. Last night he acted like he was in fourth grade, playing GI Joe or something, with those maps and everything."

"Exactly! Hey, my mom is having a coronary because she needs to use the phone. I gotta run. I can swing by after school and drop your books off if you want."

"Okay, thanks."

"Feel better!"

And I already do—one down, one to go. I try to push myself up on my bed and reach for my robe hanging on the back of my closet door, but the spins return stronger. I fall back into my pillows, wedging my old brown shaggy bear, Henry, underneath my cheek. I've had him since I was four and still keep him in my bed. He has one eye missing and several stitches to repair loose stuffing, but during one particularly horrible run with strep throat at age six, I secretly convinced myself that having him nearby helped me heal faster. I chew on Henry's tattered foot, thinking about the juice and hoping my mom brings it in something other than a red plastic cup.

* * * * *

The next time I wake up, it is 11:34. On my bed stand, my mom has left the glass of orange juice poured into one of the Detroit Tigers cups we got for free at a game last summer. The ice cubes have melted, and the juice looks thick and warm, like soup. My mouth feels dry, the corners crusty. I force myself out of bed, slipping into my robe and grabbing the cup for a refill.

From the kitchen, I can hear the TV in the family room and the cheers of the *Price Is Right* contestants. "I bid one dollar, Bob!" one contestant chirps. I hope her strategy makes her the closest to the actual price without going over. The plan works, and Bob Barker calls her up onstage to try her luck at Plinko. It's my favorite game, so I grab my fresh glass of juice and wander in to watch.

Betsi is camped out on the couch, buried underneath two afghans and staring past the TV out the window that looks into the front yard. She jumps a bit when she notices me in the room. "Hey, you're awake. Want to sit down?" she asks, pulling her legs up to make room. I shake my head and plop down in the arm-chair instead. I can feel her eyes on me, but I concentrate on the television screen. The contestant is wearing a name tag that says NANCY and a T-shirt that reads TEXANS LOVE BOB BARKER, with an airbrushed dollar sign where the s should be. Nancy stands at the top of the Plinko board with the three chips she has earned, trying to navigate the best place to drop them and win the most money.

"Everyone thinks it's best to drop the chip right above the highest money amount, but it's a mistake," Betsi says, reaching into a nearby box of oyster crackers. She drops a handful into her mouth and adds around cracker crumbs, "The trick is to find a spot off-center and let go."

She's right, but I remain silent and watch Nancy make this exact mistake, placing all her chips in the dead center above the highest amount only to watch them fall into the zero dollar amount on either side. Bob tries to act disappointed, reminds Nancy she still has a chance to win a spot in the Showcase Showdown, and leans over for his millionth kiss.

"He's such a player," Betsi says. "I can't figure out why all these ladies are jumping out of their pants for a chance to kiss old Bob. What do you think?"

I shrug. "I dunno. They're probably just excited to be on TV."

"Yeah, you're probably right." Betsi sighs. The show cuts to a commercial for dishwasher detergent. A housewife is beaming as she holds up her dinnerware, finally free of spots and grime.

"Where's my mom?" I ask.

"She ran to the store to get you some ginger ale and stuff. She should be back soon." I nod and stand back up. "Where are you going? Don't you want to see who wins the Showcase Showdown?" I linger by the chair, trying to avoid looking Betsi directly in the eye. She stares at her hands, picking at her cuticles—she's been doing that since I can remember. Mom suggested she get acrylics or regular manicures, with the idea that if Betsi invested some money into her hands, she wouldn't be so quick to destroy them. The acrylics lasted for less than a week.

Betsi takes a deep breath, as if she is about to go underwater. "Look, Presley. I hope you know I wasn't drinking last night." Her words gush out, running together.

I shrug again. "Whatever. I don't care."

"Well, I care. And I wasn't. I was just upset." Her voice trails off and then finds its way back again. "I sort of . . . broke up with someone."

I sink back down into my chair. "Really?"

"Yes, really."

"I sort of did too," I find myself confessing. "Well, we were never really going out, so not exactly. But Chris Carroll is definitely over."

Betsi nods. "Sometimes it's best to quit while you're ahead." She digs through the oyster crackers, chewing on handfuls and staring out the window again.

"Are you sad?" I ask as a cat-litter commercial plays in the background.

Betsi shakes her head. "It was for the best. We never should've gotten involved in the first place." She fidgets with her hands once more, and our eyes meet for the first time since last night. Hers are puffy and bloodshot. "Remember when I told you sometimes I wished that I could just call for a do-over? This is one of those times."

The door to the garage slams. "I'm home!" Mom calls, walking into the family room with several bags from the market. "Feeling any better?" I wonder who she is asking, me or Betsi.

"I'm going to go unload these bags, and then I'll get you some ginger ale and soup and check your temperature again. Did you get ahold of Hannah?" Mom asks.

"Oh, crap," Betsi blurts. "I forgot, she called last night."

Mom looks at me, confused. "I thought you two were together last night babysitting."

"We were," I stumble. "We just wanted to gossip about Mr. Reynolds. He dropped me off first, and he always tells weird stories on the way home."

"Okay. Well, are you going to get set up down here on the couch with Betsi, or go back to your room?"

Betsi looks at me from the couch like a puppy begging to be fed. "I think I'll stay here," I say, and Betsi smiles, giving me more than enough space to make myself comfortable.

"*All My Children* is on in an hour, you want to watch?" she asks.

"I haven't seen it in forever."

"Yeah, but it's easy to get back into—the characters never really change. They just keep recycling story lines."

"Is Erica Kane still on?"

"Of course!" she says, passing me her box of oyster crackers, the closest we can come to a white flag for now.

★ ★ ★ ★ ★

"Presley, you cannot stand by the front door all night after being sick all day. You've been running a fever, and you'll end up catching something worse than what you already have." My mother makes her argument as she cuts open packages of candy, dumping the variety into a large bowl and tossing the mixture like salad.

"But who's going to hand out candy? Peter's already left to go out with his friends."

"Betsi can take care of it—she seems to be doing better." It's hard to take my mother seriously because she's dressed up like Raggedy Ann, with a wig of brilliant red yarn and two perfect circles of blush on her cheeks. My dad is upstairs trying to fix the strap of his overalls on his matching Andy costume. They've been invited to a party being thrown by Dad's boss, who apparently takes Halloween very seriously.

"I think it's fun that you get to dress up," I tell her, wrapping my robe tighter as a chill races up the back of my neck.

"I suppose, but these heels are already killing me. Look at you—you're freezing to death. Back to bed for you." She shoos me out of the kitchen. Betsi is out on the front porch relighting the candles in the pumpkins. There are two on the stoop now, mine and hers. Betsi's black-cat design looks more like a black hole, but I'm still surprised and pleased to find it outside next to mine.

She looks up and catches me in the doorway and smiles. "Told you I'd finish." She's pulled together a makeshift costume— a black miniskirt and tight top, a headband with cat ears, and whiskers drawn across her cheeks in thick, dark eyeliner. It's crisp out but not subzero. For once we have a Halloween that won't require covering your costume with a puffy winter coat. "You better scoot upstairs before your mother freaks out. Go on, you can see everyone coming up the front walk from your window."

I retreat to my room, piling the pillows and comforter from my bed into my window seat. I keep my bedroom lights off and watch from the dark. Most of the houses on our block are decorated for the event—faux tombstones lining the front lawns, scarecrows towering above, and ghosts hanging from the tree branches. Some of our neighbors have even added strobe lights or a boom box with creepy music. Betsi has made her own contribution, playing Michael Jackson's *Thriller* from our porch. It's old but a secret favorite of ours. When it first came out, Betsi would babysit me and Peter, and we'd watch the video over and over again, trying to memorize all of the moves.

The sidewalks are full of tiny spotlights from handheld flashlights. Most of the early groups are the younger kids, chaperoned by a parent standing guard at the edge of the driveway. I think about how Halloween goes against what we were taught as kids—never take candy from a stranger. Every year around this time, the urban legends rise from the dead, and we're all reminded to check every piece of candy for razor blades or needle pinpricks from injections of rat poison. I've never actually known or met someone whose candy has been tampered with, but I bought into it for years, surrendering my bag to my parents for inspection as soon as I walked in the door.

"Trick or treat!" I hear it over and over again as Betsi hands out generous handfuls of candy to each group. My mother always overestimates how many bags will be enough, so we usually have leftovers, which she promptly hides in the cupboards above the refrigerator as if Peter and I can't get to them.

The stream of costumed kids is endless—maybe this year we won't have so many leftovers after all. I lean my forehead against the cool windowpane and drift off as the voices below chirp their "Trick or treat!" mantra, demanding a reward and threatening consequences if they are denied.

* * * * *

It's the sound of the front door slamming that wakes me up. My eyes pop open. The streets look empty now. I think Betsi must be coming in and turning off the porch light to signal to the neighborhood that our house is closed for business, but down below I see the light is still on, with Betsi's silhouette pacing back and forth on the porch. One lone trick-or-treater stands at the bottom of our steps. At first his costume looks like a hooded black cape, but it's just a sweatshirt pulled up over his head. His voice is low, and I can't make out what he's saying.

Whatever it is, it's the same tone, the same pattern, as if he's repeating himself over and over.

Betsi suddenly scampers down the stairs, still holding the bowl of candy and standing right in front of him. "You have to go. Now." Her voice is clear and forceful. His cloaked head shakes a slow "no," then he pulls back the hood and rubs his eyes. His head is tilted up, and when he takes his hand away from his face, it feels like he is looking right into my room.

It's Barry.

I duck behind the curtain, praying I haven't been spotted, and slowly peek around the edge, my heart fluttering as if I've just run sprints in gym class. Barry and Betsi are still standing at the bottom of the steps, with Betsi cradling the candy bowl in her arms. Their lips are forming words, but their voices have dropped even lower, and I can't make out anything that's being said. Barry keeps wiping his eyes. I try to identify what it is I recognize in his face and realize it's desperation.

Barry grabs Betsi's shoulders in an attempt to pull her closer to him, but she pushes him away, the bowl of candy wedged between them. He snatches it from her hands and tosses it up into the air, the pieces of candy falling down like confetti from the sky. For the briefest moment, the candy almost seems to freeze in the air around her, like numbered dots waiting to be connected in a coloring book. And as clear as I can trace the outline of the constellations in the sky, I finally see the dots between Barry and Betsi, the order in which they connect, the pattern that needs to be traced to see the true picture.

Chapter 5

Parent-Teacher
Conferences

"Looks like it's a series of storms heading our way all at
the same time—that's the cause of it." My father announces this
from behind the Metro section of the paper during Sunday
breakfast.

"The cause of what?" Mom asks, continuing to concentrate
on an ad in Arts & Leisure for a touring production of *Les Mis-
érables*. She's been using a black felt-tip pen to mark little stars
next to the reviews of movies or plays she says she wants to see
but probably never will. Peter is buried behind one of the books
from the *Lord of the Rings* trilogy. I read whatever is closest—the
label of the syrup bottle, the nutritional facts from the side of

the orange-juice carton, the coupon insert offering seventy-five cents off my next purchase of sesame-seed bagels.

"The early freeze. Says it's going to hit by Thanksgiving at the latest. I should give Tim a call and let him know. Maybe he and Barry can get the house out onto the lake early."

Every winter my father and Uncle Tim put up a shanty on Lake St. Clair for ice-fishing season. Once the weather sets in and the ice is thick enough, there is a particular alcove known as the best spot on the lake, and it quickly becomes littered with these shelters. Most are built fast and cheap with plywood, the permit number and owner name hastily painted on all four sides, per city regulations. No one puts much time or resources into construction—they just need something that will offer protection from what can be a brutal wind coming across the lake.

"Maybe it's too soon. Sometimes trying to go out too early in the season can be a mistake," my mother warns. She's right—more often than not, at least one shanty ends up sinking every season. I'm no expert when it comes to ice fishing; over the years I've just overheard Dad and Uncle Tim argue the finer points of the best time to set out on the frozen lake. They usually fish late at night or early in the morning. Barry has been going with them since he was nine or ten, and even Peter started joining the outings last year, but I've never been asked to go.

"I know," Dad tells her, standing up. "Don't worry, we've done this before. I'll give Tim a call." He tucks the section of the paper under his arm as we hear an upstairs door slam shut and the bathtub beginning to fill with water. Dad rolls his eyes. "Glad to see she's joining the land of the living before one."

"Oh, stop it," Mom snaps. "We're actually going apartment hunting today."

I stop swirling my last bite of pancake in the pool of syrup on my plate and sit straight up. "You are?"

Two weeks have passed since Halloween, and I have managed to arrange it so I am always going when Betsi is coming.

"Yes. Betsi is very insistent on finding her own place before the end of the month. She's been working for a while now and seems to think she has enough saved up. Do you want to come with us?"

"No."

"Why not? Betsi would love your opinion."

"I don't think so. I have a lot of homework."

"Well, don't forget you do have tomorrow off from school. You could always finish up then." It's parent-teacher-conference day tomorrow. Mom is scheduled to begin her rotations mid-morning. I'm golden except for math class—a C-minus on my quiz last week. I didn't even pretend to try, passing in my paper full of blank spaces.

"That's okay. I really do have a lot to do and I told Hannah I'd meet her at the library this afternoon." It's a lie but one I can make come true if I need to.

"I'm certainly not going to argue if my daughter insists on doing her homework." Mom half smiles and stands up to clear the plates.

I can hear my father reading the weather report to Tim over the phone from the living room. "Why don't we take a look at the shanty today? I can head over to your place in the afternoon. Is Barry around? He's better at troubleshooting than either of us." The bath water turns off upstairs as I hear Dad ask, "Three A.M.? What the hell was he doing out at that hour?" There is another long pause, silent except for the faint sound of sloshing water. "Jesus. Look, Tim, if you want me to have a talk with him . . . Okay. I understand. I'll be over in a few."

Dad wanders back into the kitchen while Mom finishes rinsing our breakfast plates and loads them in the dishwasher. My father tops off his coffee mug and then turns to catch my eye.

"Presley, have you noticed anything peculiar about Barry?"

I fidget with my paper napkin, peeling the corners and piling the shreds on top of each other. "I don't know what you mean."

My mother shuts off the water and turns toward me as she dries her hands with a dish towel. "Is something wrong with Barry?" she asks both of us.

"Could be," Dad says, and then gives Mom the "I'll fill you in later" eyes, as though I am still a child. They used to spell out words so I wouldn't take things "too literally." The first time I heard my father use this phrase, I was only four and didn't know what "literally" meant but assumed it had to do with the fact that I thought people meant what they said when they said it. Like when Betsi would announce with all the drama and flair of a Broadway star, "I'm so hungry, I could die," I'd rush to the kitchen, scooting a chair toward the cabinets so I could climb up on the counter and reach for something to sustain her—a box of my favorite Goldfish crackers, a handful of Oreos, a jar of olives. Or when my mother tucked me in at night and told me, "I love you with all of my heart," I thought the actual organ controlled whether or not you loved something. So one morning when I overheard Betsi sitting at our kitchen table telling my mom that she had a broken heart, I ran into the room crying, throwing myself onto Betsi's lap, terrified that there was nothing I could do to fix or save her.

"Presley, do you know if anything is going on with Barry?"

my father asks me again. Even Peter has put aside his foray into Moordoor with the Fellowship of the Ring to hear my answer.

"I—" As soon as my mouth opens, I hear the stopper from the tub being pulled and Betsi's water slipping down the drain. "I don't know. He seems fine to me."

"Hmm. Well, let me know if you start to notice anything . . . out of the ordinary."

Betsi's door slams shut again, and her hair dryer is drowned out by the sounds of an Elvis song turned up just high enough to disturb all of us. Today it's "Hard Headed Woman"; yesterday it was "Are You Lonesome Tonight?" Her selection is always unpredictable, but it's my cue: once the song starts, I have maybe a ten-minute window before she surfaces. I race to my room to gather the necessary real and fake props for my escape.

* * * * *

I started smoking the day after Halloween. I was surprised at how easy it was to buy my first pack of cigarettes. I figured my best bet was the Mobil gas station seven blocks from the school, because that was all they sold besides gas and a small selection of soda and beer. I practiced saying the word "Marlboro" in my head during the walk over, so by the time the clerk asked me, "What can I get you?" my answer rolled off my tongue as if I'd been smoking for centuries.

"Marlboro Lights."

"Matches?" he asked.

It was that simple—no asking for an ID, no raising eyebrows, no throwing me out of the store. For a moment I thought about adding a six-pack of Stroh's to the counter but decided not to press my luck.

For the past two weeks, I have been telling my parents that I am going to the library after school, or to Hannah's, but what I usually do is climb to the top of the bleachers next to the football field to smoke. This is how I pass the time until Betsi gets off of work at 5:00 P.M., and then I kill some more in case she's decided to come home long enough to dash inside, change her clothes, and head out again. Even though I never ask, my mother will often give me a report of Betsi's whereabouts when I finally walk through the door, sprayed with perfume and chewing gum to cover up my own activities. Sometimes Betsi tells my mother she is going to a group meeting; sometimes she says she is catching up with a friend for dinner; sometimes she says nothing at all.

Regardless, Betsi always slips back into our house after everyone is asleep but me. When I hear her key in the door, I make my body flat as a piece of paper, daring myself not to move just in case she comes in to see if I am awake. Most of the time she retreats to her own room, but the last few nights I've heard her pause at my door, listening for any movement to indicate that I might still be even slightly awake.

I always hold my breath until she passes.

Because today is Sunday, the field is empty, with just a few runners taking leisurely jogs around the track. I settle into my usual spot at the farthest end, last row, sifting through my backpack past the books I haven't opened in weeks until I find my headphones. Once I've slipped them over my ears, I start packing my cigarettes against the base of my palm—one of many things I learned to do by watching Betsi.

"Hey!" I hear the call right before I press play, but there's no one around or in front of me. I shrug and light my cigarette.

"Hey! Presley! Down here." I look between my feet and

into the rafters below and see Barry's best friend, Jack, standing alone underneath me.

"Oh. You."

"What are you doing up there?"

"What are you doing *down* there?"

"I'll come up," he says.

"No, don't—" I start to say, but he's already snaking his way out of the rafters and is heading up the ramp. I shrug and keep smoking, studying him as he gets closer to me. He looks like he rolled out of bed in the same clothes he slept in the night before—jeans, a well-worn T-shirt that might have said DETROIT TIGERS at one point, a sloppy hooded sweatshirt.

"You need a jacket," I snipe, exhaling. "It's getting too cold outside. What were you doing down there, anyway?"

He says nothing but marches straight for me and suddenly snatches the lit cigarette from my hand. He tosses it back down into the rafters.

"What the hell do you think you're doing?" I glare at Jack, flicking the lighter in my hand.

"You don't smoke." He says it slowly, as if there's no question that he is right, and carefully cups his hand over mine to disarm me. I wait for something else—a sarcastic barb, an insult—but he keeps his hand over mine. I can feel him looking at me, and I pull my hand back to the safety of my side.

"What could you possibly know?"

"I know enough, Presley. I know—about everything."

Our eyes lock, telling each other the same secret. We sit side by side on the bleachers, watching two ladies trying to maintain a conversation while speed-walking on the track as cars pass behind them on the road beyond the field. We sit next to each other for hours without saying a word, but in my head I begin a million different sentences, only to erase them all before any escape my chapped lips. We sit like this, our knees barely touching, our bare hands shoved into our pockets. The sky turns into a cloak of dusk, full of fat gray clouds pregnant with snow but refusing to release even a few flakes, as if once it starts, it won't know how to ever stop.

Finally, when the streetlights hum and buzz and begin to burn, Jack stands and reaches out to pull me up. "Come on. I'll walk you home."

* * * * *

"This is probably as far as I should go," Jack says a block before we get to my house. It's the first words spoken since we left the bleachers.

I nod and start to turn away but then spin back around and ask, "Do you know where Barry was last night?"

"Yes. He was with me."

"He wasn't—"

"No. I stayed with him to make sure he didn't try to go to her. She asked him not to contact her for a while—or at least that's what he told me. He's not doing such a great job honoring that request. But I stay as late as I need to, especially if he's drinking."

"When is he drinking?" I ask.

"When is he not?" Jack returns.

"Did you ever see them together?"

"No. Not in that way. But I covered for him. A lot," Jack admits.

"Why would you do that?"

"Because he loves her." He says it as if it's the most obvious answer in the world.

"They're starting to ask questions—my dad, his dad. They know something is wrong."

"You're asking a lot of questions too."

I blurt out, "I don't know if I should tell," then bite my lip, waiting for Jack's permission or denial. We stand underneath the streetlights, quiet again. The air is biting now, and Jack zips his sweatshirt, pulling up his hood and yanking the strings around his head to make the covering as tight as possible.

Jack sighs. "Don't do anything. Just . . . don't say a word."

★ ★ ★ ★ ★

Betsi's Jeep is out front. I think about turning around and sprinting as fast as I can away from the house, maybe trying to find Jack again, but I've been gone too long and I don't want my parents to start questioning me as well. I try to open the door quietly to sneak in, but I hear the TV on in the family room, the one place I have to pass through to get anywhere else in the house.

Betsi is the only person in the room, but she's not watching TV. She's following the moves of an aerobics instructor on a workout tape she has popped into the VCR. Her hair is just long enough for a short, squatty ponytail, and it looks like a fuzzy pom-pom bursting out from the base of her neck.

"Hey," she calls without stopping her routine. "Your parents and Peter are out picking up pizza. But guess what, I think I found an apartment. It's so cute I can't wait for you to see it. It has a porch and a claw-foot bathtub and it's only fifteen minutes from my job. The price is a little steep, but if I shuffle a few things around, I should be able to make it work . . ."

I fade away from her words, studying her body and trying to figure out just exactly what she is attempting to "work out." Her body is even thinner now than it was back in the summer. Her collarbone juts out from her thin white tee, and the spandex leggings hang on her frame more like sweatpants. Even her sneezes have become anorexic, a series of short, quick flutters that come and go as she completes her last set of arm curls.

"These things always end up lasting longer than I think they're going to," she says, turning off the TV with the remote and taking a swig from a bottle of water.

"Why are you working out so late?" I ask.

"I dunno, I just have a lot of energy. I can't wait for you to see the apartment. How about tomorrow?"

"I can't," I say.

"Why not? You have school off."

"I just can't," I repeat, trying to walk out of the room.

"Hey. Where are you going? I thought we could hang out before your parents get back. It seems like we never see each other anymore. I have so much to tell you—big news."

Her eyes light up. She barely takes a breath and continues. "Not just the apartment. I met someone—someone new. In my group. They say we shouldn't date anyone who isn't at least a year into the program, but, well, you know, you can't help your feelings—"

Her monologue flips some sort of switch sitting inside the cavity of my chest, opening the tunnels and floodgates and passageways to allow all the words and phrases I had pushed down into deep crevices to finally submerge. They fall out of my mouth in a flood. "Shut up! Shut up! Shut up!"

"Presley! What is wrong with you?"

"With me?" I laugh, but it is not my laugh. It's short and sharp, and I jab her with it, trying to hit her ribs, her neck, her heart. The flood continues. "I saw you."

"You saw me where?"

"On Halloween. I saw you outside—with Barry."

Betsi's face begins to fall as soon as she hears the accusation, her tight, tense, defensive eyes slowly melting into a blank stare. "I didn't mean . . . I didn't do anything," Betsi insists. "It's not what you think. I'm not what you think."

"No," I say. "You are not." And this time, when I turn to leave the room, she doesn't try and stop me.

★ ★ ★ ★ ★

The day Betsi taught me how to ride without training wheels was the first time I ever broke anything. Mom and Dad had bought me a new bike as a birthday present six months early, during the spring of third grade, so I could learn to ride and take advantage of the weather all summer long. They tricked me into believing I had to go clean out the garage, but when Dad rolled the door open, it was as if I had picked the grand-prize curtain during the last round of *Let's Make a Deal*.

The cherry bike was trimmed in white, with delicate plastic streamers fluttering off the end of each handle. The first thing I did before even taking it off its kickstand was braid the strings like pieces of hair, something else Betsi had shown me how to do. Back then I braided anything I could get my hands on—the blond tresses of my Barbies, the tassels on the chenille blankets thrown on the sofa, the cords hanging alongside the window blinds.

"You want to take it out for a spin?" my dad asked me.

"Yes! Now, now!" I begged.

"Okay, Pres. Let me just get my sweater," Mom said, turning toward the house.

"No, I want to go with Betsi," I said.

Betsi looked at my parents and shrugged. "Guess it's pretty clear who Presley loves the best." I followed her as she wheeled the bike down the driveway, telling my parents not to worry and that I was in good hands.

We decided to wheel the bike down to the park, where there were longer paths without interruption, perfect for cycling. I knew how to ride a bike, but only with training wheels. This was the first time I would try and go completely solo, with nothing to rely on but my own sense of balance and determination.

"I'm going to hold on to the seat," Betsi said, and when I started to protest, she added, "Just at first. Eventually I'm going to let go, but I'm not going to tell you when. Trust me, you won't even know I'm gone."

She was right—I was concentrating so hard on making it on my own, I didn't look back, not once after I started pedaling. The dandelions sprinkled along each side of the pathway became a blur of yellow. The braided streamer on the right handlebar started loosening in the wind. Before I could stop myself, I reached out toward the fluttering pieces to try and fix them.

I fell just seconds later—and hard. Somehow I managed to nail both my knees and my left elbow on the way down, my wrist throbbing and clearly not okay, the bike tangled above me like a cage. My fall had managed to not only rip the streamers out of one handle but to create a cluster of scratches across that beautiful cherry-red finish.

Betsi rushed over to me, muttering, "Okay. Okay. Okay,"

kneeling down next to me as I cried—not because of the pain but because of the damage I had done to the bike. "Don't move. Don't move your wrist at all, that looks like the worst of it. Um, okay. Let me think. Think, think, think."

She rummaged through her purse and came up with a small bottle of nail polish, a mini packet of Kleenex, and her hard sunglasses case. She lined everything up next to us like a surgeon organizing her tools, swiftly taking the bandana out of her hair and adding it to the group of instruments. She guided my bad wrist toward her, delicately placing the base of it on top of the eyeglass case, wrapping the kerchief around just tight enough to hold the homemade splint in place. Betsi passed me the tissues so I could attend to my other scrapes with my good hand, then she turned her focus toward the bike, unscrewing the nail polish bottle to paint over the damage I had done. Amazingly enough, the color was a perfect match—or perfect enough—and by the time she was done, the bike looked no worse for the wear except for the missing streamers. Betsi took the cluster from my hand and the chewing gum from her mouth and used it as temporary glue.

"There. As good as new," she said. "Can you stand? Because if you can't, I'll carry you home. We need to get that wrist looked at. You might need a cast, but don't worry—it'll be cool. We'll decorate with markers and get all your friends to sign it."

I nodded. "I can stand on my own," I said, doing so, remarkably calm, and holding my wrist gingerly at my side, with wads of tissue sticking to my wounds, watching in awe as my hero saved the day, right before my eyes.

Chapter 6

The Thanksgiving Day Parade

On the Friday before Thanksgiving, Hannah and I walk home from school with slow, cautious steps to avoid slipping on any black ice. My father was right—a freeze set in earlier this week, along with almost four inches of snow. It's a conservative amount compared to what we deal with all winter long, and the inches usually melt quickly. But this year the cold lingered and held on, so while the main roads were cleared and salted for safety, the borders of the streets were still marked by hard clumps of snow packed with dirt and grime. Hannah and I pause frequently to point out half-melted snowmen trying desperately to keep a sense of composure, scattered across the lawns of the neighborhood like fallen comrades left behind in battle.

"Only three days of school next week," Hannah reminds me. I nod as we navigate the sidewalk. The other objective of our leisurely walk is to kill as much time as possible so I can dodge the outing with my mother to Farmer Jack for our Thanksgiving Day food and ingredients. At this time of year, the grocery store reminds me of the slides we are shown in history class of Cold War–era Russia, with hundreds of people who look like peasants swarming the storefronts for the smallest wedge of bread, just one glass bottle of milk, a handful of fresh eggs—any piece of nourishment to keep them alive.

I shudder at the thought of the chaotic madhouse, and I wrap my ruby scarf tighter around my neck. We pass a man balancing on a ladder against his house, stringing Christmas lights from the gutters. "Isn't it a little early for this?" I ask.

"You know how it is around here," Hannah says. "Always those few houses that seem to put their lights up early and keep them up too long."

I nod again. "You're right. My dad is already dragging out the boxes of decorations from the basement. After Thanksgiving, Christmas and New Year's come like a blur."

"So who's going to be at your house for Thanksgiving?" Hannah asks, stepping over a patch of ice.

"I guess just about everyone," I answer vaguely.

Thanksgiving has always been treated as our biggest family event of the year, even bigger than Christmas or birthdays. Since Aunt Marie died, our home has been base camp for the day, and the amount of food we make ends up cluttering every open space on our dining room table. The selection of ways to fill ourselves up is endless. A roasted turkey holds center court, the stuffing spilling out from the insides sliced open by my father. The dishes of cranberry sauce are always set in the gelatinous mold of the can, down to the ridges. Arranged around the outskirts of the table are dishes that require a bit more preparation—my mother's baked carrots with freshly grated cheese melted on top, green beans with slivers of almonds added to make them slightly different from our usual weekday fare, and always a basket or two of warm crescent rolls made from dough popped out of an airtight can and brushed with melted butter while baking. Every year it is a race to see who will overindulge themselves first.

"What about Barry?"

"Yeah, Barry and his dad too. There was some talk about them going down to Florida to see Grandma Biddie, but my mom told me earlier this week that they've definitely pledged allegiance to our flag. She's really proud of this, like it's a personal victory for her in some sort of Thanksgiving Day war. I'm pretty sure it has more to do with the fact that my uncle Tim couldn't get cheap enough flights at the last minute and less to do with my mother's mashed potatoes."

"They *are* truly incredible mashed potatoes, though." Hannah speaks from personal experience—she has joined us for leftovers many times over the years.

"Good point. Still, can't I just go to Florida with you?" I ask, praying for a surprise reprieve before she leaves tomorrow. We reach the corner where Hannah heads in one direction and I follow another.

"I wish you could. Don't get me wrong—the beach is always nice. But my grandfather still asks me if I want to grab my sand bucket—my sand bucket, those exact words—and go hunt for shark's teeth and shells. I don't know why it's so hard to understand I'm too old for that now."

"Actually, it sounds kind of nice. I used to spend a lot of time with Grandma Biddie, doing the same thing on the beach down the road from her." A snapshot appears in my head from a trip we took years ago, back when Peter was still just a growing bump in my mother's stomach. My father had decided we needed one more getaway from the bitter weather between Christmas and New Year's, before it would be too late for my mother to fly in her condition.

Betsi had come with us. As a Christmas present, Dad had flown her in from Toledo, where she was on break between her first and second semesters of college. My mother had told me psychology was "what you study when you want to help understand others and their problems." I remember nodding as if I knew what she meant, and continuing to color in my *Sesame Street* book, making Grover green even though I knew he was blue.

Betsi let me bury her on the beach during that trip. Back then her long hair was bottle-blond, piled high atop her head. I packed the sand tightly around her, then outlined her neck and chest with broken bits of shell, pressing the coral and white pieces deep.

"Don't try and get away," I told her.

"I won't," she said. And then, "Can you keep a secret?"

"What's a secret?" I asked.

"It's like when I tell you something that's very special or important to me, but you can't tell anyone else."

"No one?" I said.

"No one," she responded. "Are you ready?"

"Yes," I told her, kneeling in the sand, the sun trying to work its way through the Coppertone on my back.

"I flunked out of school. I'm not going back," she whispered, scanning my eyes for a response.

Instead of words, I responded by tracing an outline of where I thought Betsi's body was hidden underneath the sand, all the way down to her feet, and back up toward her exposed face. Once I'd made the circuit, I finally spoke. "Can we go in the water now?"

She nodded. "Help dig me out?" I grabbed my bucket and shovel to free her.

I was only five years old.

"Presley." It's Hannah's voice, and the snapshot evaporates. "Where'd you go?"

"Nowhere," I say. "Have fun. And don't forget to send me a postcard!" Hannah has a knack for finding the most out-of-date, ancient postcards in gift shops across the country. She raises her hand in acknowledgment as she starts to walk away, but then stops, turning to face me again.

"Hey, Presley. What about Betsi? Is she coming home?"

The sound of her name feels like a frigid slap of wind.

"That's what I've been told," I say, waving goodbye once more before I turn away, praying that my mother has already left for the store and taken Peter with her. Just to be safe, I take baby steps the remaining four blocks, counting each movement and adding one thousand to the end of every number until my driveway is in sight and, thankfully, vacant.

* * * * *

The morning after I confronted Betsi, she disappeared, leaving behind only scant traces of evidence that she had ever been in our home and in our lives again—one of her barrettes abandoned next to the bathroom sink, her disposable razor on the ledge of the tub, a carton of the vanilla-flavored creamer she used in her coffee still sitting in the fridge. I put the barrette and the razor in a Ziploc bag and held it over the kitchen garbage but changed my mind at the last minute, deciding to hide the bag in my closet, in a shoe box full of ribbons I'd won over the years from various spelling bees and science fairs.

I checked the creamer's expiration date: October 14, a day that had long since passed. I stood at the sink dumping the curdled cream down the drain, taking in the sour smell, letting it seep into my nose, my head, my memory.

As I did so, my mother walked into the kitchen, lifting her car keys off of one of the hooks by the phone. "Hey, Pres. I'm running a few things over to Betsi's new place. She's signing her lease right now. You want to come?"

"No, thanks," I said, disposing of the empty carton.

"What's that horrible smell?" my mother asked, scrunching her nose and wrinkling the skin under her eyes.

"Nothing. Just spoiled milk."

When I looked up at her, she noticed the tears in my eyes.

"Presley! What's wrong?" she asked, searching my face for more clues.

I bit my lip and swallowed my words.

"Oh, Pres. It's okay. I know everything," she said, pulling me into a hug. "And it's okay. It's perfectly normal to feel like this."

"It is?" I asked, wondering how she knew and how she could remain so calm, collected, as if we were in church listening to the second reading according to Luke.

"Of course it is. But just because Betsi doesn't live with us anymore doesn't mean you'll see her any less, or that she loves you any less. I know how much you look up to her, Pres. And Betsi knows it too."

My body became a rigid board of wood as I started to back away from her.

"You sure you don't want to come? Betsi would love to show you her new place."

"No. I'm okay. Everything is fine now," I said, wanting to believe it.

* * * * *

The Wednesday before Thanksgiving, Mr. Underwood tries to trip up our math class with another pop quiz, but for once the problems are all easily solved with standard formulas and equations. The cafeteria serves up its best Thanksgiving Day–themed meal: thick, fat turkey slices covered in yellow gravy, outlined with ice-cream scoops of mashed potatoes and green beans floating in a baby pool of water.

With Hannah in Florida, it's just me, Jill, and Karen at the table today. "That food looks dreadful," Karen says, sounding a little like royalty. "How can you stand it?"

I stop midbite and shrug. "I dunno. It's comforting?"

The girls look at me, waiting for more of an answer, but right now it's all I have to offer.

Jill snorts. "Hey, Presley, there's your boyfriend."

I look up, expecting them to still be hammering away at what we now call the Chris Carroll Incident, but it's Jack walking through the lunchroom, and he's heading right toward our table.

"Ladies," he says, nodding in the direction of my friends. "Sorry to interrupt, but you mind if I borrow Presley for a moment?"

Before either Karen or Jill can answer, Jack lifts my arm, but gently, guiding me away from their shocked stares and the puddle of yellow gravy I was trying to lose myself in.

"What are you doing?" I hiss through my teeth.

"Just trust me. Walk with me," he says through his own forced smile.

"Where are we going?"

"Away from here," he says, and the words are exactly what I need to hear.

* * * * *

Jack drives me to the edge of Balduck Park, beyond the rusted swing sets toward the edge of something we all grew up calling a lake. It's really just a large, moldy pond that turns cold enough every winter to qualify as ice but isn't nearly sturdy enough to skate on. We sit in his maroon Pontiac Grand Am, watching the ducks teeter on the barely frozen water, and I wonder why they are still here, trying to hold on to something that is already changing into something else.

"What are we doing?" I ask for what seems like the millionth time.

"We are taking a break."

I wonder if the principal has called my parents. "What made you think I'd want to take a break with you?"

"You're here, aren't you?" he argues.

"That wasn't my choice."

"Wasn't it?" he asks, softer now. He's right—I was grateful when he swooped in and took me away.

We sit in his car, staring at the ducks and watching the sun fall in between the barren branches of the elm trees that surround the water, listening to old Bruce Springsteen songs playing on a cassette that keeps looping back to the beginning. I wonder if he is going to try and make a move on me, but Jack remains perfectly still, his fingertips resting lightly on the knees of his weathered blue jeans, his car seat leaned back for more comfort and space. I am the one who finally edges in—first just a half inch, then another, then another—until I am close enough for my head to fall on his shoulder.

He doesn't protest. We sit like this until the sun disappears into the faintest traces of pink and it's once again time for Jack to take me back to a place I used to call home.

* * * * *

Later that Thanksgiving eve, Mom lobbies the rest of us to catch a movie and "get out of her hair," but when Dad and Peter pick a sci-fi film, I decide to stay home. The kitchen is dark except for the halo of light shining down over the sink, where my mother stands scrubbing potatoes, softening them underneath a light stream of running water.

"Mom?"

"Hmm?"

"I wanted to talk to you about something." My words are staccato, my voice rusty, as if I haven't used it for days.

"Sure. Just give me a sec. I need to finish up these potatoes so I can get them in the oven and out of the way."

"Can I help?" I ask, though I expect her to insist, per usual, that she prefers to work alone.

My mother canvasses the situation, her eyes scanning the stack of thick, sturdy Idaho potatoes. She sighs, pushing a lock of her hair from her eyes with her wrist. Then she glances at the clock and allows defeat to sink in, her shoulders falling, her head nodding slowly.

"Okay. Yes. Yes, you can. Will you start peeling these potatoes? Here, take this peeler and bowl over to the kitchen table."

"But I can't do them the way you do," I argue, taken off guard, forgetting for a moment the big announcement I had been preparing to share. When my mother peels potatoes, it is serious business. They are left completely naked—not a scrap of skin on the tough ivory bodies.

"That's okay. Actually, why don't we leave some of the skins on? That's how your grandmother used to make mashed potatoes when I was your age."

"But that's not how you usually do them," I say.

"I know, but sometimes things taste better when you leave them closer to the way they were."

I nod, even though I don't believe a word she is saying.

"Here, let me show you." She takes a scrubbed potato in one hand and holds it over the bowl, peeling sections away to form a sort of zebra potato. "The excess skins will boil off," she explains in a voice that sounds fit for a professional cooking show. "Then, when we mash the potatoes, the skins will mix in, just bits and pieces but enough for you to taste."

I try it with a fresh potato and make it look identical to her demonstration spud.

"See? You've got it! I really appreciate this, Pres. I don't know what I would have done if you hadn't come in to be my little helper." My mother returns to her station at the sink, carving out the eyes from the potatoes before scrubbing them clean. "What did you want to talk to me about?" she asks.

There are at least twenty-seven potatoes that require my newfound handiwork.

"Nothing," I say. "It can wait."

* * * * *

Peter is oddly obsessed with parades, and on Thanksgiving morning, he hits the mother lode: the televised local parade held in downtown Detroit, followed by the annual Macy's Thanksgiving Day parade broadcast from New York. I can understand the fascination with the Macy's parade, because it is usually peppered with celebrities and singers. But the floats are more or less the same every year, and they're all sponsored by this corporation or that. I walk into the family room, still in my pajamas, and spot Peter curled up on the couch watching the Big Bird float struggling to get by in what seems like a blizzard falling on the streets of New York City.

"Doesn't this just bore you to death? It's like one big commercial," I comment, reminding him of my opinion even though he didn't ask for it.

"Presley," he says, scooping handfuls of Golden Grahams into his mouth from the box on his lap, "you're missing the point."

"And what's that, exactly?" I ask, amused by Peter actually attempting to argue a point.

"The Macy's parade isn't about the biggest float or the best marching band. It's all leading up to the most important thing—Santa Claus."

"Santa Claus? Peter, are you saying you believe in Santa Claus again? Because I hate to break it to you, but that's just some retired senior citizen getting paid to spend time in a red velvet suit and fake beard."

"Of course I don't believe in Santa Claus. Not like he's a real person. Besides, it's scientifically impossible to make it around the world to everyone's house in one night," Peter instructs.

"Thanks for the lesson, but I still don't get it."

"It's not about whether Santa Claus is actually real. It's about what he represents—the idea of the Christmas Spirit, this brief period of time when people believe that anything is possible, no matter how bleak things look or feel."

I open my mouth to protest and then promptly clamp it shut, watching the North Bloomington High School marching band follow the carved path in the slush and snow with a jaunty version of "It's the Most Wonderful Time of the Year."

* * * * *

The family begins to show up shortly before the Detroit Lions kick off their annual Thanksgiving Day game. My father has already gridded a sheet of paper for the football pool. Squares go for a dollar apiece, and I buy five, marking my initials in spots scattered across the graph. At the end of each quarter, we check to see who has the square that corresponds with the current score. The numbers across the top half represent the Lions, and the numbers down the side represent their opponent— this year, the Chicago Bears.

When Uncle Tim and Barry arrive, they shed their coats, and Tim pulls out a twenty-dollar bill. "I'm feeling good about the Lions this year. Sanders is unstoppable."

"He's still young. How can you be so sure he'll come through?" Barry snaps, grabbing a handful of mixed salted nuts from a bowl on our coffee table.

"Never underestimate the power of the underdog," my father interjects. "Come on, Barry, why don't you help me fill out these leftover squares."

Aunt Helen arrives with my cousins and even Uncle Richard this time—I guess lawyers get Thanksgiving off. She asks me to help her carry in paper bags of wine and 7-Up. "For the kids," she explains, as though I'm unclear. Mom is bent over peering at the turkey in the oven.

"Don't keep opening the door, it'll just take longer," Aunt Helen scolds, as if she has her own cooking show.

"Yes, I know, I'm just keeping an eye on it." Mom sighs, turning off the oven light.

"Where's Betsi?" my cousin Kristen asks, pouring herself a large glass of soda without ice. "She promised she'd show me how to do a French manicure."

"Aren't you a little young for manicures?" I say under my breath.

"I'm sure she's on her way," my mother says.

"I don't think we've all been together since the cottage. Is that possible?" Aunt Helen asks, helping my mother fold cloth napkins and slide them into fancy silver rings.

"That was a long time ago," I blurt out.

"It wasn't that long ago, Presley," Mom points out. "Just a few months."

"Yes, but everything is different now." Once again my words come out without warning, before I realize what sentence I am forming.

Mom and Aunt Helen exchange a quick glance they think

I don't see, but they don't reply. Kristen pauses briefly midsip and then adds more 7-Up to her glass so it is once again full.

"I . . . guess I'll put the napkins on the table," I say, gathering the rolls bound together by only the thin, simple curve of silver.

* * * * *

Mom added the extra leaves to our mahogany dining table so there would be enough room for everybody. But even with the extra space, the spots are nearly overlapping, the outside salad forks of one place setting butting up against the soup spoons of another. I wanted to sit near Barry, but he has taken the seat at the farthest corner. With Uncle Tim on one side of Barry, that leaves only the head of the table, which is Dad's traditional spot. I anchor myself in the middle, so I can still keep an eye on Barry but have a better chance of second helpings of the best dishes.

Mom starts bringing the food to the table, spacing out the covered tureens. I can hear the buzz from the kitchen, where Dad is slaying the turkey with his electric knife; no one else in the house is allowed to touch it, not even Mom. Earlier this morning, I asked Dad why he's so in love with the gadget.

"Because," he explained. "It does exactly what it's supposed to do—quickly. It lets me get to the core of what I really want."

The turkey is sliced, light and dark meat arranged on my mother's large white porcelain platter, and set on the table last. We are all seated except for Mom and Dad, who hover in the kitchen having a whisper conference. Only two empty seats remain at the table, both of which had been reserved for Betsi and, as she confided in my mother when they didn't know I was listening, the person she has called "the best fuck of my life."

My mother's reaction was surprisingly calm and blasé. "Betsi," she said, sighing, "that's not exactly the best reason to get swept up so quickly in someone else."

"That, dear sister, is a matter of opinion," Betsi said.

Whoever this new guy is, the one thing he's not is in our dining room, and neither is Betsi. Aunt Helen stares at her watch, although there's a large grandfather clock right behind her. Uncle Richard uses the edge of the tablecloth to wipe off his glasses. Uncle Tim cracks his knuckles. My other cousins begin to fidget, especially Kristen, who whines just loud enough for everyone at the table to hear: "Can we start passing the dishes?"

Barry stares at his empty plate.

I catch Peter's eye. We both know very well what cue needs to be given before the meal can proceed with parties still absent. Our parents' whisper conference turns into a swirling hum building into a crescendo of my father declaring, "We will not wait for her anymore." He storms in the room and takes his seat, unfolding his napkin and placing it in his lap. My mother follows slowly like a dog that's been scolded and sinks into her chair.

"Now," my father finally says, "who wants to say grace?"

* * * * *

The call from Betsi comes as we are clearing the dishes, the phone ringing just as Dad drags Uncle Tim and Barry into the garage to look at the new lantern he bought for their ice shanty. They are planning to go to the lake this weekend, early, during that time when the light of day hasn't quite started to peek from the horizon. "Now we won't have any problems seeing what we're doing. Trust me. This is the best light you can buy," I overhear him boasting.

I know immediately it's Betsi on the phone, because it's just my mother and me in the kitchen, but Mom turns on the garbage disposal to muffle any transcriptions of her conversation. The cordless phone is tucked into the crevice between her neck and shoulder so she can use both hands to push the scraps down the drain. I refuse to touch other people's left-behind bits without giant yellow rubber dishwashing gloves, but my mother is fearless about it—usually. Right now she stops completely, and the garbage disposal makes that empty sound like it's clearing its throat and looking for more.

Mom flips off the disposal in time for me to hear her say, ". . . in Vegas, while we all sat here waiting for you. I know you're happy, but really, Betsi, I just can't talk to you right now. Be safe." My mother's hands are dripping all over the buttons of the phone as she more or less hangs up on her sister.

"You're going to ruin the phone," I try to tell her, but she ignores me, dropping it back in the cradle without wiping it off.

"Presley—"

"I don't want to know." My words come out hard, serious— final. Remarkably, she nods in agreement and then presses start on our dishwasher, which is packed with more dirty plates and glasses and silverware than one household should ever have.

* * * * *

"Hey, Presley."

It's Barry's voice at my bedroom door. He raps gently when I fail to respond, and continues. "Can I come in for a sec?"

"Sure," I say from my window seat. We already said our

family goodbyes at the front door. I fled immediately afterward to avoid any further discussions with Mom, just in case she tried to share more details about Betsi's impromptu Vegas trip. Down below, I can see Uncle Tim's truck idling in our driveway, my dad leaning in to talk, shoving his gloveless hands into his pant pockets to shield them from the wind that is beginning to pick up again.

"Sorry, am I interrupting?" Barry asks politely, as if I am a stranger.

"No, I was just reading," I lie. There's a book open on my lap—it's the one Barry gave me for my birthday, *Tender Is the Night*. But I've been rereading the same sentence for the past five minutes, the words on the page replaced with images of Betsi in Vegas feasting on all-you-can-eat shrimp and feeding quarters into slot machines with the best fuck she's ever had.

"What do you think?" Barry asks. My face is blank. "About the book. Do you like it so far?"

"Oh! Yes, I do. Though I'm not really sure why Dick Diver is so dedicated to his wife. She seems so unstable."

He nods. "But he loves her. And it's not really her fault."

"Isn't it? I guess I thought she sort of thrived on the craziness, the drama, around her." I slide my finger into the book to hold my page. "You were right, though. He writes about being in love in a way that's different from anything I've ever read."

"So hey, I meant to give this to you before I left tonight." I expect to see another book in his hands, but he's holding his varsity jacket. He extends it to me as if it's wrapped in a bow.

"Your jacket?"

"Yes. I want you to take it."

"Why? It's got all your varsity pins on it, your letter, everything."

"I know. It's just—things are tough—right now. You know, with Lyndon and the team and my grades . . ." His voice trails off.

"And other things too, right?" I dance around specifics.

Barry sinks into my desk chair, clutching the jacket in his hands like a rope. "Why didn't she come tonight, Pres? I really needed her to be here."

I sigh. "I think she just got . . . tied up. I don't know."

"I do. She's with someone. That guy. I know it." He stands up again, walking toward me with his offering. "I need to straighten things out, like a do-over. So please. Take it." Now Barry is the one whose voice sounds hard and serious, his eyes certain and final.

"How about I just keep it for you? For a little while?" I ask. "Like a loan."

"Okay, Presley," he says, handing me the cluster of leather and wool. "Okay." He starts to leave but pauses in the doorway. "I don't think it was her fault—the wife in the book, Nicole Diver? I think Dick just thought he could save her and save himself. Maybe he just lost himself along the way, and by the time he realized it, it was too late to go back and change things." I keep my eyes focused on Barry's varsity pin attached to the front pocket as he adds a quick "See you," and then he is gone. I am left clutching his two gifts—a jacket representing so much of what he's accomplished and a book I am struggling to finish, full of words and ideas I might never understand.

* * * * *

My back is to my bedroom door when my father pokes his head in to say good night. Barry's book is still open in front of me, though my progress has been minimal since he left: fourteen pages. I tried to switch locations to speed along the process, but moving from the window seat into my bed just made me more tired. Underneath my covers, I'm still wearing my favorite pair of gray corduroys and my eggshell-colored cardigan, but if my dad notices, he doesn't say a word.

"Whatcha doing?" he asks, sitting on the edge of my bed.

I turn over toward him. "Just reading."

"You were awfully quiet tonight."

I shrug. "The turkey made me tired."

"Yes, well, that's the tryptophan."

"Right. I can never remember the name of it."

"I noticed Barry came back in to see you?"

"Oh . . . yeah."

"Did he want anything in particular?"

"No, not really." Barry's varsity jacket is on the desk behind my father, but he doesn't notice. I stare at the cover of *Tender Is the Night.*

"Is there something I should know, Presley?"

"No." I sigh. "He just wanted to ask me what I think of the story so far." I hold the book up to Dad so he can see what I'm reading.

"Oh. Anyway, I came up here because I have something for you."

"What is it?" I ask, now feeling neither calm nor sleepy.

My father reveals what he has been concealing in his left palm—a nearly perfect wishbone, plucked and cleaned dry. "Do you want to make a wish?" he asks, holding the bottom of one end.

I stare at the U-shaped bone with a thousand possibilities held in its tip, thinking how this will be the first time in years that Betsi is not holding one end and I the other.

Dad reads my mind. "I know she's not here, but you should still get to make your wish."

"It only comes true if I get the end with the tip at the top."

"Well," my father says, patting my leg hiding underneath the blanket, "why don't you give it a try."

I sit up and grab the free end, close my eyes, and pull. The bone snaps easily, just a quick pop, and when I open my eyes and see what I am left holding, I believe for just the briefest moment that my wish might come true.

Chapter 7

Ice Fishing

On Thanksgiving night, I fall asleep with the broken wishbone on my bed stand and dream that I am treading water in Lake St. Clair in the middle of the night. There is snow on the banks of the lake, but the water is as warm as a bath, and I can feel the strands of algae tickling the bottoms of my feet. My legs cycle in the water to keep me afloat, but they are heavy sand-bags, and I blame too much turkey for the exhaustion. I squint and try to spot any signs of cars approaching in the distance on the road. There is nothing—just the light from the full moon skipping across the surface.

My mind tells me I should start heading toward the shore, yet my body refuses to cooperate, and my legs continue to circle in the same spot, stuck in a pattern and moving at a much slower speed. I think maybe if I dip below the water for a moment, it will break the spell and set me free so I can swim to safety. I stop fighting and let myself fall under, closing my eyes, because at this time of night, I won't be able to see anything.

Hey, Presley. Down here.

The voice is so close it sounds like it's coming from inside of my ear. I am only inches below the surface, but the words startle me enough to spring me waist-high out of the lake. My body lurches toward the shore, arms crawling through the water at remarkable speed in an attempt to save me from whatever was waiting at the bottom.

     ★ ★ ★ ★ ★

It's way too early in the morning for phone calls, especially for a holiday weekend. The shrill rings roll into one another without an answer, then begin a second round. My eyes pop open. From my bed, I can see that the streetlights are still burning outside, competing with the early daylight. I lie under my covers with my quilt pulled up to the bottom of my chin, listening to the phone cry out over and over again, begging for someone to pay attention.

The sky begins to take on shape and color, a red glow seeping into my room and swooping across the walls. I wrap my blanket around my shoulders and shuffle closer to the window.

The phone is still ringing.

There are two police cruisers parked outside.

It's the busiest shopping day of the year, I think.

I watch the officers get out of their cars. There are four of them, one woman and three men, bundled in state-issued parkas with a silver name tag on the left breast. The female cop says something into her radio as they all begin closing in on our front door. I wander out of my room, and as I head for the stairs, I hear my parents' closet door sliding on its tracks and imagine my father is looking for his robe. I am already at the bottom landing when the phone rings are finally cut off by the sound of my mother's muffled "Hello?"

I open the front door before any of the police officers have taken one step onto our porch. The tallest cop, a man with broad shoulders and a mustache and a tag that says POLARSKI, takes lead.

I wonder if he remembers our house from the fire in the fall.

"You shouldn't be standing in the doorway without any shoes on," he says.

I look down at my bare feet as I hear my father approaching behind me. As the winter wind sneaks in and whips around my ankles, the police dispatcher's voice crackles through Polarski's walkie-talkie: "The body has been recovered."

"Presley," my father says as the feedback squeals through the house. "Go upstairs. Now."

I scurry away from all of them as Polarski turns down the volume and mutters back some sort of confirmation. When I get to the top of the stairs, I can hear my mother weeping in her room. I duck around the corner in case she decides to come out, and slide down against the wall with my blanket just outside my bedroom door. I hear Polarski providing details to my father, and though the officer tries to keep his words low, I pick up enough bits and pieces even over my mother's sobs.

Truck found near lake. Headlights left on. Ice shanty. Accidental drowning.

When I realize who they are talking about, I crawl back toward the shore of my bed, wondering how, in a million years, Barry could ever forget how to swim.

Chapter 8

The Last Monday in November

    I can hear signs of life downstairs—mostly the opening and closing of things: the front door, the refrigerator, the stove, the garage. There are voices as well, though they are unidentifiable, overlapping into one constant hum like the dehumidifier my mother puts in my room when I have heavy congestion. The visitors start showing up early in the morning, and they rotate through the house during the day, their cars pulling up and parking in our driveway or on our street. I hear people stomping the snow off their shoes in our front hallway, and then, after a while, gathering their keys at the end of the day and warming up their engines to leave. But I never see their faces.

It has been two days since I moved from my bed. Trays with triangles of peanut-butter sandwiches, bowls of chicken soup, and glasses of milk begin to stack up untouched on my nightstand. When I hear my mother's footsteps approaching, I close my eyes and listen to her watching me. Eventually she sniffles or sighs and gives up. After I hear her leave, I count to a hundred before opening my eyes again, just to make sure she is gone.

The milk she brings me begins to curdle within twenty-four hours of exposure to the open air. In the middle of the second night of my self-imposed exile, I hear my mother return. She whisks away the milk from my room, as if it never existed in the first place.

* * * * *

After two days in my room, I try to remember how to sit up so I can go downstairs and demand my parents take me to the hospital. I will insist a surgeon open my chest, because I'm certain he will discover that my heart looks nothing like the vibrant, shiny, pulsating core we were shown in biology class. Instead they will find crumbles of coal, or maybe just an empty cavity where my heart used to be. When I come out of surgery, the doctors will explain that we can register for a donor but that the prognosis is bleak, because the waiting list of people with a broken heart is endless and I have just stepped in at the end of the line.

* * * * *

The morning of the third day, it is my father who comes into my room. I smell his aftershave first, then feel his weight sitting at the end of my bed, but I remain completely still, as if I have just been caught in one of the games of freeze tag we used to play at the cottage in the summer, waiting until someone passes underneath my legs to free me again. Barry was the only one who could manage to sneak around and put me back into play before our parents would tell us to come in for the night.

"Pres. Are you awake?" my father asks. "Honey, I know you're awake. It's time. Today it's time. Your mother picked out some clothes for you. The shower is free. We set clean towels out on the counter, a fresh bar of the lavender soap you like. Make sure you dry your hair all the way. The temperature is dropping, and your mother doesn't want you catching a cold."

He talks as if I am going to get ready for a piano recital.

"Your mother thought it would be nice for you to do one of the readings at the service. We've made a photocopy of the section. It's very brief, easy. Nothing to get worked up about. It's just a piece of paper." He sighs and adds quietly, "I'm sure your uncle will appreciate it."

I answer with silence.

* * * * *

"Presley. It's time to go."

It's not a request anymore. His declaration becomes gospel, just like when he determined Thanksgiving dinner would be served with or without Betsi.

I open one eye but avoid making direct contact with my father's. My clock radio tells me it is 8:32 A.M.

"Did it snow?" I ask, my voice small and hoarse.

"Yes," he tells me. "It snowed a lot, Presley. It's been snowing for days."

Sarah Grace McCandless

* * * * *

I stay in the shower until the hot water becomes lukewarm against the back of my neck, then turn the water off and heat myself with the steam that has collected in the bathroom as the water disappears. I wrap my freshly washed hair in a thick baby-blue towel, tying the belt of my winter robe around my waist until it is snug and tight. My outfit for the day waits for me on the back of the bathroom door—my black wool skirt and matching cardigan wrapped in plastic fresh from the dry cleaner; a pair of stockings draped over one shoulder; a strand of my mother's pearls wound around the neck of the hanger.

I rub away the steam to uncover a clear spot on the mirror, studying the lack of color in my face, the circles engraved under my eyes. Like my clothes, other necessities have been laid out next to the sink—deodorant, comb, gel, hair dryer, a compact of blush, a tube of sheer maroon lipstick. It's the one item in the group that is not mine: the tube is too expensive, the department-store kind in a gold and red case. It's not my mother's either; she never strays from the rose or coral family. This color is much too dramatic for her tastes.

I pop the cap off the tube and twirl it up. The tip is sharp, angled, curved just slightly at the end. It's the only clue I need.

Betsi has returned.

* * * * *

I find her behind our garage, sitting on an overturned bucket in the snow, smoking a cigarette and pulling the collar of her black leather coat closer to her neck. There are mascara smears underneath her eyes. Her hair is pulled back fiercely, knotted in a small tight bun at the nape of her neck. She doesn't see me at first, and I watch her whispering something to herself that I can't make out.

"Hi." It might be the first time I've spoken to her since she moved out.

"Oh, Presley!" She exhales, her tossed cigarette sizzling in the snow. Her embrace nearly knocks me over like a linebacker, her arms circling and imprisoning mine before I can decide whether or not I want to raise them. If she remembers anything about our last interaction, she doesn't let on.

"I just can't believe it, I can't even think straight, it's all happening so quickly, the accident, the funeral—"

"You're tan," I blurt out.

"What?" she says, releasing me.

I step back and take a harder look. "You're tan," I repeat. "Your face."

"Oh. Well, it's probably from Vegas. I don't even know. Where is everyone else? Are we going?" she rambles, tapping out another cigarette from her pack.

"Almost," I say. I repeat what I was told in the kitchen. "Dad is warming up the car. Mom is making plans where to meet with Aunt Helen, and then we're supposed to go."

"Will you sit with me, Pres?" Betsi pleads, her frantic eyes dashing around my face as if it's a racetrack and she can't find the finish line. She slips the cigarette into her mouth, but it's backward and she's about to light the wrong end. "Please? I really need you. Everyone else has been walking around like, like, I don't know, just not *saying* anything, and I can't stand it." Betsi realizes her mistake and drops the wasted cigarette on the ground. "See? I can't even smoke right. I just don't know if I can make it through this day without you. I can't even imagine walking into the funeral home."

Her bloodshot eyes finally lock with mine.

"I . . . haven't seen him yet," she whispers. "The body."

"We should go wait in the car," I say, turning and walking away from her words.

"Yes, we should," she repeats, scampering next to me, slipping one of her leather-gloved hands into my own, as if I am the mother and she is the child being walked to her first day of school.

* * * * *

Betsi sits in the backseat between me and Peter, who is dressed in a blue blazer usually reserved for weddings and baptisms, with a navy-and-kelly-green tie clipped to the collar of his pressed shirt. He's holding an old issue of *Newsweek*—it's our father's subscription—and for once I wonder if his reading materials are simply a prop.

Betsi leans more toward my side, so I press myself as close to the door as possible, resting my head against the window, the glass like a sheet of ice next to my cheek. Betsi's gloves are in her lap, and she fidgets with a blue rhinestone ring on her right hand, twisting it around her slim finger and rubbing the top of the stone. I sneak a look at her face and see she is moving her lips again, repeating something with only the faintest sound escaping. The car radio is silent, so she is not singing along with any music the rest of us can hear.

"What day is it?" I ask, watching my father in the rearview mirror as he drives and tries to keep his eyes on the road.

"It's Monday, Presley. You know that," my mother answers. Even though I am the one who just emerged from the cocoon of my room this morning, it is my mother who seems to have transformed over the past few days. Her normal layer of worry has been covered by a sheet of calm. She seems out of place, like a Christmas tree that's been left in the living room well past the New Year. "We're almost there," she adds, as if I am impatient and eager to reach our final destination.

When my father turns the corner, we are still three blocks from the funeral home, but there is already a stream of cars coming from both directions and pulling into the parking lot. Clusters of people are hovering outside on the shoveled sidewalks, and I start to recognize faces from school.

"There are so many people." Betsi breaks her silent mantra to mutter exactly what I am thinking.

"Barry has a lot of friends," my mother says. "He's very popular."

"He was." It's Peter talking.

"What's that?" my mother asks, flipping down the visor mirror to double-check that every hair is in place, her lipstick fresh.

"He was. He was very popular," Peter quietly corrects her.

Betsi and I stare at him. My mother continues fixing herself, mumbling, "Hmm," which I guess is supposed to qualify as some sort of response. My father parallel-parks on the street and remains silent.

"Why don't you all head in? I'll be right behind you," he says. "Betsi, can I talk to you for a minute?"

The sun hides behind fat puffy clouds, refusing to come out and melt the snow packed around us. My mother ushers Peter and me toward the funeral home. I turn to look over my shoulder, expecting to find my father yelling at Betsi, but I see her nod and pull out another cigarette, which she lights correctly this time—and then hands to my father. He takes a long drag, holding the smoke in his lungs for a moment and then letting it disappear into the winter air. He starts to take another drag and sees me watching him. I turn away and keep up with my mother's strides, brisk and even, as if we are marching into the battle of our lives.

* * * * *

The inside of the funeral home looks like a school assembly but smells like a combination of canned air freshener and rubbing alcohol. It seems like nearly everyone from the senior class is here, and most of the faculty. Word must have spread quickly over the past few days, even with the holiday break. Outside of the room where the service will be held, there are clusters of junior and senior girls weeping softly and anchoring themselves in each other's arms. I see Liz, the girl who stopped Barry in the hallway on the first day of school, and overhear her lie to her friends, "We were so close. He was going to ask me to prom." I pass behind her and make my way toward Hannah, Jill, and Karen, who are waiting in what seems like a receiving line. Karen embraces me first, hard but quick, followed by Jill, who has wads of tissue crumpled in the palm of each hand.

Hannah hugs me last and longest.

"I thought you weren't coming back until tonight," I say.

"My parents flew me out yesterday on standby," she tells me. "We called—all of us—but your mom said you were . . . unavailable."

"We're so sorry," Jill offers. "I can't believe he's gone, everyone worshipped him so much." Karen nudges her with an elbow, but Jill's pause button is out of order. "It's just so awful, the drowning, all of it—"

"Jill," Hannah says cautiously while Karen tries to plunge daggers from her eyes into Jill's throat to make her stop talking.

Jill swallows her sentence but adds, "I just meant I hope he didn't suffer."

"Presley!" Betsi's voice storms into the conversation followed by the rest of her. "There you are. Oh, girls, it was so nice of you to come." She wraps her arm around mine, marking me as her territory. I notice that her coat is closed but off by one button. "Pres, shouldn't we go in now?"

"I think I want to stay out here with my friends for a little longer," I say.

"But you promised you'd walk in with me and stay by me." Betsi's voice is almost a whine, and it briefly feels like we are having an argument over who can sit at whose lunch table.

"It's okay, Pres," Hannah says, trying to diffuse the scene Betsi is creating. "We'll find you later."

"I'll walk in with you too, Pres." I don't need to turn around to identify the voice. I feel Jack place his hands on my shoulders, and I let them guide me out of Betsi's grasp and into the next room. Betsi and the girls fall into formation and follow.

My mother is near the front, pointing out an arrangement of lilies and lilacs to my aunt Helen. "Breathtaking," I hear her say. "Aren't they?"

Peter lingers near her, obviously trying to decide where to sit. The rest of the cousins have already filled in the second row. My father and Uncle Tim are planted in the front. My father holds his shoulders stiff and rigid, while Uncle Tim's shoulders

Sarah Grace McCandless

are beginning to cave until Dad places his arm around them as an anchor.

And then there is Barry. When I first see him lying in an open casket in his pressed suit, it looks like he's sleeping, as if I could walk up to him and poke him in the ribs until he's forced to giggle and say, "Good one, Pres. You got me."

* * * * *

"'Behold,'" I announce to the room. "'I tell you a mystery.'"

I have been assigned to read a passage from Corinthians that was photocopied and handed to me on a single piece of paper. I smooth down the corners of the sheet and continue. "'We shall not all sleep, but we shall all be changed.'"

The words begin to blur in front of me. I shake my vision clear. "'We will all be changed,'" I repeat, "'in an instant, in the blink of an eye, at the last trumpet. For the trumpet will sound, the dead will be raised incorruptible, and we shall be changed.'"

My legs wobble behind the podium as I race through the rest. ". . . 'Where, O death, is your victory?'" I fold the paper back into a rectangle, looking up for the first time at the faces that have been staring at me. The only eyes in the room not on me are Barry's, still closed. I wait for him to wake up, slowly stretching as he rises and yawns, asking, "Are you finished yet?"

* * * * *

Barry was always known as the napper in our family. It didn't matter if he was on a plane or at fireworks on the Fourth of July. Most of the time his naps would come without warning—one minute he would be wide awake, participating

136

in the conversations around him, and then within a matter of seconds he would be fast asleep, a bemused expression on his face as if he was already dreaming of a joke he might tell us later in the day.

I remember watching him sleep years ago, during Betsi's twenty-first birthday party in May. Mom offered our house for the party, and Betsi invited a bunch of old friends from high school. We set up a tent out back and the grill to barbecue packs of hot dogs and hamburger patties seasoned with Lipton's onion soup mix. My father had agreed to man the grill, but when Betsi's friends started showing up, they concentrated mostly on drinking all of the beer stashed in giant blue coolers around the backyard, even the cans packed in ice at the very bottom. The family members invited to the party segregated themselves toward one end of the yard, watching Betsi's friends reenact moments from their senior spirit week and prom, as if they had happened the day before.

Betsi had, of course, chosen Elvis as the sound track for her party, but when her old high school boyfriend Patrick showed up, she started pulling out tapes of a band named Chicago, then one called Boston, and I wondered if all the bands her friends liked in high school were named after cities. The more cans that disappeared, the louder the crowd became, singing along with the songs and even slow-dancing in our backyard. Mom was swaying a little bit too, holding Peter, who wasn't old enough to walk yet. Dad had grilled way too much food, and the burgers and hot dogs lined the racks, shriveling into unrecognizable forms. I started to head toward Betsi's group because they were clearly the most fun, but my father told me to stay away from the smoke and to go ask Barry if he wanted something to eat.

Barry had stationed himself in our new hammock, anchored between two elm trees in the farthest corner of the yard. The noise from the party was inescapable, but Barry was fast asleep, swinging back and forth slightly, as if he were in his own outdoor cradle. I quietly pulled one of the folding lawn chairs closer, settling in and positioning my paper plate carefully over my lap to catch any mustard from my hot dog so it wouldn't stain my white party dress. I chewed on my soggy bun and listened to Chicago sing about taking away the biggest part of me, watching Barry's chest rise and fall, and wondered if he was dreaming about his own first slow dance, just a few years away.

★ ★ ★ ★ ★

"There is nothing harder."

These are the first words I hear when I fade back into the room where everything is taking place. It's Uncle Tim's turn at the podium. He's armed with a speech he prepared himself, and this is how he begins.

"There is nothing harder," he tries again, "than losing a child."

After one complete sentence, his words evaporate and his face crumples. My father glides up to his side and eases Uncle Tim back into his seat. My mother offers him a travel-size tissue pack from her purse but continues dabbing her own eyes with a monogrammed handkerchief. Peter sits next to her, reading the pamphlet printed with our hymns and responses. Betsi is next, and she is trying to sit on her hands to make them stop shaking. Jack and I round out the end of the row. I let him hold two of my fingers but not the entire hand.

My father replaces Uncle Tim at the podium and says, "We want to thank everyone for coming today and giving our family such tremendous love and support. You are all invited to join us at our house following this service." He gives out our address in case there are some who don't know.

I pray that most of them decide not to show.

★ ★ ★ ★ ★

"I'm going to call the school in the morning and tell them you won't be in," my mother says to me as she hangs up the skirt and sweater that I left wadded on my bedroom floor.

"Why?"

"It's okay to take a few extra days for yourself. Your teachers will understand."

"I don't need to," I say, reaching over to set my alarm clock.

"It's probably a good idea."

"I don't *want* to," I explain.

"Well. Why don't you sleep on it and decide in the morning."

My mother kisses me good night on my forehead. After she closes the door, I turn off the light on my nightstand, and in the darkness, I let my tears fall for the first time. They saturate my pillowcase as my fingertips graze the cover of *Tender Is the Night* tucked secretly underneath. If I can fall asleep into the pages, I think maybe I might find him there, still waiting for me.

Chapter 9

Let It Snow, Let It Snow, Let It Snow

The high school hallways are wallpapered with posters announcing the upcoming winter formal. I walk from class to class like the Ghost of Christmas Past under the glitter and tinsel and Magic Marker sketches of mistletoe. It has been two weeks since Barry's funeral, and the way other students react to me varies between someone nominated for prom court to an outcast with the plague. Senior girls I've never spoken to stop me in the hallway to tell me "I love your skirt." It's their version of "I'm sorry." I've found three notes in my locker in the past week from boys in the sophomore class, telling me they will take me to the dance. Not asking me but telling me, as if they are bound by honor or obligation. Then there are the people I thought I counted as friends, like Karen, who refuse to look me in the eye, afraid of catching the disease known as grief.

When I dart into the girls' bathroom between classes, I sit on the lid and tuck my feet up so no one can tell I am in the stall, listening to random voices talk about *the accident*.

The only good part is my teachers. I feel guilty for taking advantage of them, but they refuse to ask me about homework assignments. Every quiz I've been given since Thanksgiving has come back to me marked in regular blue ballpoint pen (no bright red felt tip) with a note along the lines of *Will retake after the first of the year,* even the tests I scored 80 percent or better on, as if I could've done differently under ideal circumstances.

I want to turn the quizzes back in with my response scrawled next to their remarks: *Do you really think things will be better by then?*

* * * * *

The school newspaper comes out every Wednesday, and this week the story about Barry finally makes the front page. My first-period teacher slides me an early copy as morning announcements come through the overhead speaker. The students sitting around suddenly become remarkably rigid, pretending I am not there, eyes forward, as if they are in drivers' ed.

Barry's senior photo is blown up so big that it runs above and below the fold, his name and the bracketed dates—year of birth, year of death—serving as the headline. Inside, there is a four-page insert covering every possible topic from coping with the death of a young peer to safety precautions when fishing on the ice. The editor of the paper is a feisty senior named Justine

Huse who's had her eyeglasses perched on top of her head every-time I've seen her. She's already received word of early acceptance to Northwestern's journalism program and makes sure to announce this within the first few minutes of all conversations. She has also left three messages for me, two at home with my mother and one with my school counselor, requesting an interview for this special edition of the paper. I sent my handwritten decline directly to the journalism adviser, Mr. Bozzi, sneaking into the faculty office and sliding it into his mail slot. Regardless, I notice a *Special Thanks to Presley Moran* tagged on the end of the main story.

The journalism students normally leave copies of the paper in bundles outside the cafeteria and other classrooms for the teachers to pick up and distribute. I skip third period and gather as many bundles as I can carry in my arms, taking them outside behind the bleachers. With a matchbook left over from my smoking days, I throw lit matches at the copies until there is nothing left but a pile of black soot, kicking snow over the ashes just to make sure the fire is out.

* * * * *

Betsi has been camped out on our couch since the funeral. All traces of her tan have disappeared, and each day when I get home from school, it seems like she is in the same position as when I left that morning. Every second or third day, while the rest of the family is eating dinner, Betsi drags herself upstairs to take a shower or at least run the water. Sometimes when she comes back downstairs, she's in the same clothes and her hair is still dry, so I'm not sure what she actually does up there.

Since Barry's funeral, my mother has been insisting that we all sit down and eat as a family every night, not just at the kitchen table but in the formal dining room, with place settings. Apparently Betsi is excused from this declaration, but the rest of us are expected to be in our spots promptly at 6 P.M. Mom explained that it was important to spend time together and talk about our days, but most nights we've just been passing dishes and listening to my mother fill the empty air with stories that have nothing to do with our family—the steaks on special this week at Kroger, the new wire-and-lights reindeer decorations available at Meijer, how long it took to get a parking spot at Lakeside Mall during the holiday shopping season.

Tonight is Taco Night, and there are tiny bowls of garnish on the table for our creations. Peter is using the soft shells and making tortillas, carefully adding each layer in a precise order: refried beans, rice, ground beef, cheese, lettuce, tomato, and one dollop of sour cream directly in the center. My father keeps his tacos simple, hard shells with lettuce only, scooping the other items onto his plate as separate side dishes. Mom has combined the ingredients to make a taco salad of sorts that sits nearly untouched on her plate. She takes a breath after her recounting of an article in the Sunday paper on how people celebrate New Year's Eve across the globe. Before she can move on to the next subject, I jump at the opening.

"Mom?" I say, sprinkling extra shredded cheddar cheese on my taco to make it look like I am eating.

"Yes, Presley!" she exclaims, relieved that someone else is taking a turn.

"Why is Betsi still here?"

Dad pauses midbite with a forkful of Spanish rice but then continues eating, leaving Mom to respond on her own.

"What do you mean?"

"She's staying here again, right?" I ask, as if I don't know.

144

"Just for a little while."

"So what about her apartment?"

"Well, right now she's still paying rent there, but she's staying with us . . . for the company."

"What about her job? At the dealership?" I'm really on a roll now.

"She's on bereavement leave," my mother says, moving her fork around her plate, rearranging her food but still not making a dent in it.

"For how long?" My taco has become a base for the cheese mountain I've built over it.

"She'll probably go back to work after Christmas." Her responses are quieter now.

"That seems like a long time."

"Yes, well . . ." Her voice trails off. I wonder what story she's trying to come up with next.

"I don't know why she's getting special treatment. She's not even really related to Barry, you know."

My father finally speaks. "Presley." His voice is stern and even. "Stop playing with your food."

I look up from my taco project and notice the tears tracing my mother's cheeks. She sets her fork down on the edge of her plate and pushes her chair back from the table, mumbling, "Excuse me," before fleeing the room. My father sighs and tells me to clear the table and clean the kitchen before I go to bed, my punishment for asking too many of the wrong questions.

* * * * *

The next day Jack is waiting for me outside of the girls' locker room after seventh-period gym class. Unfortunately, Mr.

Lyndon isn't one of the teachers giving me a break right now; we just finished indoor sprints across the waxy basketball court for the last forty-two minutes. I didn't even try to shower or fix myself up after class, just throwing my street clothes back on with my cheeks still flushed and my hair plastered against my forehead. I wrap my scarf around my neck and throw my backpack over one shoulder, hoping I can make it from the locker room to the school doors without another round of awkward hellos or silent stares from people I don't know.

"Presley," Jack calls out after I walk right by him.

I jump. "You scared the shit out of me."

"Sorry," he says, his eyes darting back and forth. "You got a minute?"

"Yeah, but I have to get out of here. Walk with me?"

He nods, fidgeting with his brown wool cap.

"What's wrong with you?" I ask as we shove through the doors, the stark air making my sweaty face instantly cold and clammy.

"Nothing," he says, keeping up with my pace. We've walked three blocks in the direction of my house before he speaks again.

"I think we should go together to the winter formal tomorrow night," he blurts out, fast, like a tongue twister.

I stop walking.

"Really," he says.

I think it's the first time I've ever seen Jack look embarrassed.

"Look, I need to get out and do something, or I'm going to go crazy. If I go with anyone else, they're either going to act completely strange or too nice. Do you know what I mean?" he asks.

"Yeah, actually, I do—I know exactly what you mean."

"So you'll go?" he says again.

"Is this like a date?" I can't believe I just asked that.

"No! It's . . . a thing we're going to do." His response comes a little too quickly, and I'm surprised at the bubble of disappointment that breaks over me. I throw out my next thought to cover any signs of my reaction.

"I . . . I don't have anything to wear." It's the closest thing I can come to saying yes.

"I'll pick you up at seven."

Jack shuffles down the street quickly. During the rest of the walk home, as I'm trying to figure out what just happened, I remember that Betsi will be there when he arrives. I daydream about tying my bedsheets together and throwing the makeshift rope out of my window as a means of escape so Jack won't see her and I won't have to explain the look he has in his eyes when he does.

* * * * *

"Oh, Presley! Your first date!"

My mother's reaction to my news about the dance is more like I just won the Miss Teen Michigan crown.

"It's not a date—it's just friends going to a school thing together. A bunch of us are meeting there," I lie. There was no way to avoid telling my parents about the dance. I'll be missing Friday dinner and out later than usual, which meant getting permission for an extended curfew.

"Did you talk to your father?" she asks, rinsing the chicken cacciatore off of our plates. I had waited to approach her until after dinner, making sure I ate every bite and nodding more than occasionally during her monologue to butter the path.

"Not yet. I wanted to tell you first." I put the pitcher of iced tea back in the fridge.

"Well, I'm sure it'll be okay. As long as you two aren't out too late."

"It's just Jack, Mom. It's not a big deal," I tell myself as much as I am telling her, rearranging the magnets on the fridge. My mother still uses the neon alphabet magnets she first bought when I was maybe three years old, to help me learn how to spell and read.

"What will you wear?" she asks. "I guess we don't have time to shop for anything new, do we?"

"I'll find something," I say, arranging the letters: X—M—A—S.

"You know, you could ask Betsi to borrow something of hers."

"No." I spell the word as I say it. N—O.

"Why not?"

"We're not even close to the same size," I blurt, arranging the three I's to make a triangle.

"Oh, of course you are. You two are almost exactly the same build."

"What are you talking about? Betsi is much skinnier than I am. And at least two inches taller."

"Pres, you can't see yourself the way everyone else does. People tell me all the time how alike you two look. You'll probably look even more like her the older you get. It's not such a bad thing to be compared to the girl you said you always wanted to be."

I disconnect the triangle to borrow one of the I's.

G—I—R—L.

"I'm not like her at all," I mumble, breaking apart all of the plastic words on the fridge, the letters once again becoming nothing but a random clutter.

★ ★ ★ ★ ★

I end up raiding Hannah's closet after school on Friday. She pulls out at least fourteen different combinations, spreading them out on her bed and hanging some of the possibilities off of her curtain rod for evaluation.

"I think it's nice," Hannah says quietly.

"This?" I ask, holding up a white blouse.

"No. That Jack is taking you."

"Oh. Yeah well . . . we're just trying to do something that feels normal." I slip my arms into a dark green dress, running my hands over the shiny fabric and wondering if it's too much. Hannah is still looking at me. "It's not like *that*," I tell her.

"Okay, okay," she says, standing up to help with the zipper. "But I think he'd be glad you two were going together," she adds. We're both becoming experts at avoiding the use of his specific name.

I settle on a simple black skirt that swings a bit when I walk and a red cashmere sweater. When I get home, I shower and leave my conditioner in for an extra five minutes to help make my hair as soft as possible. I settle in front of the dresser mirror, wrapped in towels and examining the lines on my face and the circles under my eyes.

"I could help you, if you want."

Betsi hesitates in my doorway, pulling on a lock of her hair that has fallen free from the short, messy ponytail holding the rest together. She's wearing boxer shorts and a white tank top with a light orange stain near the collar.

"Aren't you cold?" I ask her, ignoring her comment.

"No," she says, examining her bare arms and legs as if she just realized she had them.

I turn back to the mirror and start squeezing the water out of my hair into my towel. She waits in my doorway as I drag a comb through the snarls.

"Why don't you let me dry your hair? I can get it really smooth and straight, the way you like it."

"That's okay, I can do it myself."

"Please," she says. "I want to."

When I look at her, she is shivering in the doorway, so I nod, extending the comb her way. She approaches slowly at first, as if waiting for me to change my mind, but then takes the comb and finishes pulling through the tangles. Betsi rubs styling cream through the ends and then plugs in the hair dryer behind the dresser. She tackles my hair in sections with a large round brush, pulling each segment tight and running the heat of the dryer right up against the roots. The lamp on my dresser flickers occasionally as it struggles to share the current with the dryer, but Betsi stays focused, stopping momentarily to step back and assess each section before moving on to the next one. I watch her reflection in the mirror as she moves around me, trying to remember how to make things look perfect.

* * * * *

I keep watch from the living room window, and when I see Jack's car coming down the street, I throw out a quick "Bye!" to my family, racing out the front door before they can respond. Jack is pulling into the driveway as I scamper down the sidewalk, not caring if I fall on the ice.

"I was going to come to the door," he says as I slide into the passenger seat.

"That's not necessary," I say. "Let's go."

"Your parents are going to think I'm a jerk. I need to go inside and at least say hello."

"No, don't worry about it," I argue. "Really!"

Jack turns off the ignition.

"Betsi's still there. She's staying with us again," I say.

He pauses, then starts the car again and reverses out of the driveway.

I exhale with my victory, rubbing my hands together for warmth and thinking about the gloves I left behind on the kitchen table.

"You look nice—" he starts.

"Shut up, Jack."

He laughs for a minute, short and nervous, and then mumbles, "Well, you do."

We drive in silence the rest of the way, listening to the traffic and weather report. *The southbound lanes on I-75 between downtown and the Ambassador Bridge are closed for overnight maintenance; chance of flurries, sixty percent.*

* * * * *

The dance is set up in the school cafeteria, tables cleared and chairs stacked in the corner, with plastic punch bowls and cookie trays sitting out in the spot where they usually scoop lunch onto our trays. It's a schoolwide dance, so there are students from all grades clustering underneath the colored Christmas bulbs strung from the corners and ceiling, burning across each end of the room. The DJ has two poinsettia plants on his table, and he is playing a Madonna record to, as he announces, "get this party started." It works, at least with some of the girls, who squeal and start bouncing frantically, singing along with every word.

"I'm not sure if this is my scene," I lean over and yell into Jack's ear over the music. We are standing in the back of the room, side by side like cardboard cutouts.

"Maybe that's a good thing," Jack yells back. "Your scene right now sort of sucks." He's wearing a red tie with a blue button-down shirt and gray slacks. When I find Hannah, she will probably tell me he looks cute. I'd agree with her but never admit it.

This is not a date, I remind myself. This is a distraction.

"Are you thirsty?" he asks.

"Not really."

"Do you want to sit for a while?"

"Not really."

"Maybe we should dance," he suggests.

"But it's a fast song," I point out, mortified at the thought of fast-dancing with him—or anyone—right now.

"Yeah, but it doesn't have to be." Jack takes my hand and leads me right into the middle of the crowd, pulling me close and turning me in slow circles with him. I turn my face slightly toward him, smelling the traces of menthol shaving cream left over on his cheek and neck. Our timing is completely off from what's going on around us, and I know we're making everyone stare more than they already were, but right now all I care about is having someone else take charge of things, even if it's only until the end of the song.

* * * * *

Jack parks a few houses back from mine, per my request, but I can see my parents' bedroom light is on. They're waiting up to see whether or not I will make curfew.

"Thanks again," I say.

"For what?" he asks, flipping the stations to try and find something other than Christmas carols.

"For letting me hang out here and run the clock out. I'm trying to take advantage of the extra thirty minutes they gave me."

"So they upped the ante on the curfew, huh?" he says, settling for a Commodores song on 100.3 FM.

"Yeah, you should feel really special." I try to deliver this with as much sarcasm as possible, but when I check Jack for a reaction, he's staring at the steering wheel like he's watching TV.

"How much time do you have left?" he asks.

I lean over and check the digital clock on the dash. "Twelve . . . no, make that eleven minutes."

"Pres?"

"Uh-huh."

"They asked me to clean out his locker earlier this week . . . so your uncle wouldn't have to do it."

I pause, listening to Lionel Richie singing "Sail On." "I didn't know that."

"I waited until after school so I wouldn't have to talk to anyone or explain what I was doing . . ." His voice trails off, and his eyes wander toward the house across the street, where the path is lined with waist-high plastic candy canes.

"What is it?" I ask.

Jack turns back toward me, and for just a moment his face looks blue from the moonlight falling across it. He leans down and reaches underneath the driver's seat, pulling out a spiral notebook. "Most of the stuff I found was textbooks that belonged to the school. There weren't any pens, or erasers, or calculators—nothing—just the textbooks and this notebook." He pauses briefly. "Most of it is blank."

"Most?" My voice starts to quiver. "You know what, I should go."

"But you still have a few minutes."

"Not really," I stammer, gathering my purse and buttoning my jacket. "I'm sorry, I really have to go." I reach to open the door.

Jack grabs my shoulder. "Presley. Did Barry say anything to you before—I mean, did he give you anything?"

"I don't know what you're talking about," I mumble, trying to shake myself away from his reach.

"Did he give you his varsity jacket?"

My hand freezes on the door handle. "How did you know that?"

"Because it's in this notebook. He made a sort of . . . list."

"What do you mean, a list?" I ask, and as the words come out of my mouth, I want to catch them and stuff them back inside, but they break into the air around us like bubbles blown from a wand dipped in a jar of soap. Jack sits silently, leaning his forehead against the notebook, which is propped between him and the steering wheel.

I deliver my verdict in a voice that is a block of ice. "It was an accident."

As I leave, I slam the car door hard enough to make the icicles in the trees behind me shatter and fall to the ground.

* * * * *

Barry's jacket is buried at the bottom of my closet under a stack of sweatshirts, behind my roller skates and next to a shoe box filled with every note Hannah and I have passed since third grade. I sit on the edge of my bed facing the closet door, hands neatly folded in my lap, knees together, both feet firmly planted on the ground as if I am in church.

The marigold-trimmed cuff of the navy jacket sleeve peeks out at me from underneath the pile. I lurch forward and give it a tug, yanking the jacket free. It's not the way the coat looks or feels in my hands that overcomes me; it's the smell, a mix of pine needles and campfire that is so distinctly Barry. I close my eyes and hold the jacket in my hands like a deflated balloon, sliding my hand into one pocket. I pull out a pack of cinnamon gum with three of the five sticks left, a stub from Tiger Stadium dated last spring, a book of matches from the Freeman Dodge dealership where Betsi works, and three crumpled dollar bills. I place everything on my bedspread in an even line, like instruments on an operating table.

In the other pocket, there is only one item—a piece of notebook paper, folded twice. I drop it on my bed like I just pulled out a body part.

I sit with all of Barry's things and watch the numbers on my clock go deeper and deeper into the night. When I finally open the note, there are two words inside, printed neatly in Barry's handwriting. I stare at them until they blur into an optical illusion and then come into focus again.

I'm sorry. I'm sorry. I'm sorry.

Chapter 10

Graceland

What awakens me is her breath—a puff of red wine mixed with tobacco. After opening my eyes, I try to back away slowly until I notice hers are closed. She is next to my bed, her face only inches from mine, whispering the same jumble of words I still cannot decode. She's planted in the spot where I used to kneel for my nighttime prayers, and she stays there even when I reach over to the bed stand and turn my table lamp on to the lowest setting. The haze spills across my bed where I had fallen asleep surrounded by Barry's things. She doesn't seem to notice the clutter and continues repeating her chant, the words tripping over each other in a hush.

"Betsi?" I ask. "What are you doing in my room?"

Her eyes snap open. She looks around as if she doesn't

remember how she got herself here. My blinds are closed, and though the morning hasn't made its way into my room yet, my clock reads 10:12 A.M. I wonder how I slept so late.

When she speaks, her voice is sloppy. "You need to get your things."

"What things?"

"You need to pack. We're leaving soon. I'll help you." Betsi pushes herself up, using my bed for leverage. Underneath her leather jacket, she's wearing a black dress cut low in the front, more evening than office wear. On high heels, Betsi staggers toward my desk, where my backpack sits, and I notice runs in her matching black nylons, racing up the back of both legs. She fumbles with the zipper on my bag for a minute until she figures out how it works, and then she pulls it back in one quick swoop. The entire backpack falls open, and all of my books come crashing to the floor, with pieces of loose-leaf paper fluttering down behind them.

"What are you doing?" I am sitting up in bed now, trying to keep my volume low but failing.

"I told you," Betsi slurs. "We hafta pack. Gotta get on the road soon." She's still holding on to my bag and seems oblivious to the mess she's made as she wanders back to my dresser, yanking open every drawer. She finds my purple bathing suit crumpled in the back of one and throws it into the backpack, along with a rolled tube of gym socks and a pair of jeans I'm too big for but haven't gotten around to throwing away. She rummages around on my closet floor and adds a single sneaker but not its mate, then my travel umbrella, hanging from a cord on the back of my desk chair. She zips the bag shut again.

"Oh," she says, trying to steady herself. "You should get your toothbrush too. Your mom would want me to make sure you brush your teeth. Every night. Every night, that's what you're supposed to do."

"You're drunk," I say.

"No, I'm not," she answers. It's the same voice I used when I was six and guilty.

"Yes. You are. Please put my things down."

"Okay, I am!" she says, bursting into a cascade of laughter. "But it's okay, Presley. Really. Come on, now! Don't look at me like that. I just want you to like me again. I like you liking me." She starts singing the phrase: "I like you liking me, I like you liking me—"

"Stop." I want to yell it at her, but my voice cracks, and it comes out sounding broken. I try a different tactic. "We aren't going anywhere," I say, like my dad would, as if I am in charge.

"Of course we are!" She starts singing her words again. "Do you wanna know? Do you wanna know?" She drops her head and shakes her hair, then lifts her head back up. Her eyes are glassy and her lips are pursed as she announces in a low southern drawl, "We're going to Graceland, baby!"

She flops down on my bed, crushing Barry's jacket and the note beneath her.

I remember how to shriek now.

"Get up! Get up! You're ruining him! You're ruining him!"

I push her off my bed, and the wine in her system keeps her limber as she tumbles easily to the floor. I wonder where my parents are and why they aren't bursting into the room. As I wait for them to come in and take charge of the situation, I gather Barry's things in my arms and listen to Betsi on the floor.

"Humpty Dumpty sat on the wall, Humpty Dumpty had a great fall," she chants softly, still curled up in a ball. At first it sounds like she's giggling while she speaks. She starts to push herself up, and her staccato laughs become coughs and then turn into cries as she tries to go on. "All the king's horses and . . . all the king's people . . . and all of the people . . . and no one could put Humpty back together again." Tears run down her cheeks, taking her mascara hostage with them.

I get out of bed and place Barry's things in the bottom of my closet, then close the door. My arms are shaking as I slip on my robe over my pajamas and slide my bare feet into my house slippers. I watch Betsi on the floor, crumpled and sobbing, and reach my hand out toward her. "I'm sorry I pushed you."

She looks up and takes it, but once she's steadied herself, she brushes me away.

"Fine," Betsi says, her voice dull. "If you won't come with me, I'll go by myself." Her walk across my bedroom is more confident now.

I follow, trying to keep up. "You can't drive," I tell her, racing down the stairs behind her. She ignores me, grabbing her purse from the hallway table. She tries to keep her balance as she sifts through the bottom of the bag for her car keys, pulling out a flurry of receipts and matchbooks and loose change, all of which she dumps on the floor to find the keys.

The rest of the house is strangely quiet and empty. I try to think of a way to stall her, closing my eyes and praying my family will pop out from around the corner and yell, "Surprise!" so I can find out that all of this has been one big misunderstanding.

* * * * *

I am standing behind Betsi's car so she can't back out of the driveway. I am still wearing my slippers, and the snow has seeped through them quickly. I cannot feel my toes.

"I'm not going to tell you again, Presley. Get out of the way." Betsi is sitting in the driver's seat, trying to warm up the engine of her Jeep. She pops her head out of the window to give me this warning. The air is so cold, there's a good possibility the Jeep won't start, but I am not taking any chances. When she opened the door to get in, I spotted at least three empty wine bottles rolling around on the floor. I doubt she'd make it out of our driveway or the street before wrapping the Jeep—and herself—around a lamppost or tree.

I'm also a little afraid she might run over me, so I yell back, "I changed my mind. I want to go with you." The smoke coming out of the window from her lit cigarette is her only response. "Unlock the passenger door?" I ask.

After a moment, I hear her click the door open.

I limp toward the car door on feet that are now frozen ice blocks, and lift myself into the passenger seat. Betsi has a fourth bottle of wine nestled between her legs, and her cigarette dangles from her lips. She rolls the driver's-side window up until there is just a crack of outside air. The engine spits and coughs but can't seem to clear its throat. Betsi taps the accelerator and balances her cigarette in the ashtray as she takes a swig from the open bottle. The cork is wedged between the dashboard and windshield next to several others. A minicorkscrew dangles from her key chain.

"I just need to give the engine another minute. Then we can get going," she says, her speech much slower now.

"Do you have the map?" I ask. It's the only thing I can think of as my eyes dart toward the side mirror, wishing for a glimpse of my parents' car coming up our driveway.

"Map? What map?"

"The map to Graceland. How will we know how to get there without it?"

Betsi thinks about it for a minute, taking another drag.

"I bet Peter has a map," I tell her, my feet thawing in the car's heat. "We could go back into the house and look in his room. It won't take long."

"I got it. Hold this," she says, handing me the bottle of wine. "There's an atlas in the back here somewhere." She climbs through the space between us, rifling though a stack of magazines and clothes on the floor behind us. Her body blocks me from the ignition, and before I can reach beyond her, she is settling back into her seat with a tattered atlas.

"It's not very far, I think," Betsi mumbles, flipping through the book until she finds the two-page spread of the United States, with highways running across the land like arteries. "We're going here," she explains, pointing to the capital of Missouri, a good three states away from her true target.

"No, Betsi. Here," I say, moving her finger to Memphis, Tennessee. She nods, the ashes from her cigarette sprinkling onto the pages like a burst of snow flurries.

"We need to pick up Barry too."

"We can't pick up Barry," I tell her, the water surfacing in my eyes.

"We'll make room," she insists, taking the bottle back and coating her throat with wine again.

"No, Betsi. Barry's gone," I say. "Barry's dead."

It's the first time I've said it out loud, and the words hang in the air between us with her clouds of smoke.

The engine grows tired of trying and sputters to stillness.

"Yes. He is," she says. "And I can't call do-over, can I?"

Betsi closes the atlas and lets me turn off the car. I slide the keys out of the ignition, in case she changes her mind again, just as my parents pull up behind us. Peter is with them, and I watch in the side mirror as he jumps out of their car while Mom and Dad unload paper bags of groceries. They approach us on both sides of the Jeep, their arms full of food for the holidays, their eyes becoming narrow and puzzled as the scene between me and Betsi comes into focus.

There's a fresh layer of snow across the neighborhood, light and fluffy and barely touched by harsher elements. Peter lies on our front lawn to make snow angels, his arms and legs fluttering furiously as if he might grow wings and fly away from here.

"Tell them," Betsi says as my parents tap the car windows for a response. "Tell them everything."

Chapter 11

New Year's Resolutions

"Maybe I should leave out a sweater or two, in case the weather changes again," my mother announces. She holds up her yellow cashmere cardigan, inspecting it for snags or holes.

"I think we're okay for now," I tell her, pulling at the fray on my denim shorts. I am sitting on the edge of her bed as she packs our winter coats and heavy wool sweaters into a cedar chest with mothballs tucked into each corner. Before placing each item inside, she folds it precisely to maximize the storage space. I am waiting for her to finish so we can start dyeing the hard-boiled eggs set out in a bowl on the kitchen table. Easter is in one week, and I have opened the kit from the drugstore, lining up all of the colored tablets next to the wire holders used for dipping.

"Are you going to put the chest in the attic?" I ask.

"Eventually. But I guess I'll wait until your father is here so he can lift it." She moves on to a forest-green cable-knit pullover, tucking the arms underneath the body.

"Will he be home tonight?"

"I'm not sure." She starts to sigh but catches herself and clears her throat instead. "They're making good progress on Tim's deck, now that it's staying light out later." Dad has been spending most of his time after work and on the weekends at Uncle Tim's house. Mom says he's just keeping Uncle Tim company and helping with repairs so the house can go on the market by summertime, but I know better. Even when Dad is here, he usually sleeps on the couch. On the nights when he doesn't come home at all, our mother makes a big production out of telling me and Peter how much work is left to get the house in shape.

"Your father says the problems are structural—in the foundation—places that need reinforcement, she'll say, repeating exactly what my father told her and sounding like a building contractor. "I bet he just crashed out on Uncle Tim's couch. Poor thing," she'll add, as though she's his mother and not his wife.

"Presley," she says now.

"What?" I say, pretending like I've been paying attention the entire time.

"Does this still fit you?" my mother asks, handing me a cream-colored cowl-neck sweater.

I spread it out on my lap. "This isn't mine."

"It has to be yours. It's not mine."

"No," I repeat. "It's not."

"Oh," she says, realizing her mistake. "Well, then. I guess

I'll just set this aside." She tucks Betsi's sweater into the top dresser drawer and continues searching through her closet for other items to put into storage. A slice of the sweater sleeve edges out from the corner of the drawer, preventing it from closing all the way, and for a moment I wonder if my mother did that on purpose so she would remember it was there.

★ ★ ★ ★ ★

Later that evening, I hear my father come in through the back door. Peter and I are sprawled in the family room with homework on our laps, a rerun of *Three's Company* playing on the TV.

"Hey, kids," Dad tosses out as he darts upstairs, and right then we know it's just a change-of-clothes pit-stop visit. Our mother follows him anyway.

I count to five and then tell Peter, "Don't change the channel. I'm just running to the bathroom." When I get upstairs, I peek around the corner into my parents' bedroom and see my father packing several pairs of underwear, socks, and a windbreaker, as if he's going away for camp.

"Are you staying for dinner?" Mom asks, hopeful.

"Tim and I were going to grab a couple of sandwiches and watch the hockey game." I retreat farther back in the hallway so I can still listen to the rest of their conversation, but I keep the nearby bathroom door cracked open in case I need to hide.

"I see." Her voice falls several stories.

"Kath, don't. Don't do that. Don't look at me like that. He needs me right now. He doesn't have anyone else left."

"Well, your family needs you right now too." My mother mumbles this, but I'm surprised she says it at all.

"I would've expected you, of all people, to be a little more understanding," my father responds, sighing with every word. It's the same voice he used when I brought home a report card last year with a C in math.

"It's Betsi, isn't it?" Mom asks.

My father refuses to confirm what she already knows.

"I'll see you in a few days," he tells her, zipping his duffel bag closed. I slip into the bathroom and shut the door before he passes so I won't have to watch him leave us once again.

* * * * *

On Saturday afternoon, I meet Jack for burgers at Telly's and tell him about the latest exchange between my parents. We take our usual counter seats, and Jack asks for refills on our Cokes.

"Are you mad?" he asks, licking a drop of ketchup off his thumb.

"At who?" I take a bite of the bacon cheeseburger, the juice running across my fingers.

"Your dad, I guess."

"No. Sort of? I can't really blame him right now." I wipe my hands off on a napkin and begin attacking my fries as though it's been days since my last meal. "Mostly I just feel bad for my mom."

"She's still talking to Betsi, right?"

"Yeah. Sends a letter every week, sometimes a package with books and magazines and stuff. My mom says she's going to make the drive for a face-to-face visit next month." This time around, the treatment facility is two hours farther away than the last one, and much more rigid. "They allow visitors now," I add. "I'm sure my dad will be thrilled to hear that."

"Are you going to go with your mom?"

I take an extra-large bite of my burger to avoid answering. Jack does the same, and we chew in silence for a while before he moves on to the next question.

"So what do you think he expects? That your mother will never speak to her own sister again?" he asks, and I don't think he necessarily disagrees with the idea.

"In a perfect world, probably." On the other side of the diner, I spot some of Barry's old football teammates crammed into a booth. "Those guys keep looking over here."

"Let them look," Jack says.

"Don't you know them?"

"They were more Barry's friends than mine," he admits. "Hey, Pres?"

"Yeah?" I say, reaching over to help myself to Jack's fries.

"I don't think it's possible."

"What's that?" I ask, wondering if I can sneak in another order of fries.

"A perfect world."

★ ★ ★ ★ ★

Despite Betsi giving me permission to tell all, she was the one who ended up confessing to my parents. As soon as they saw the wine bottles, my father set his grocery bag down on the hood of Betsi's Jeep. "Go inside," he told me, "and get into a hot bath before you get frostbite. Go on, now." My mother shooed Peter away to a friend's house down the street and started helping Betsi out of the car.

"Not again, Betsi," I heard my mother say. "Not again."

I followed his orders and filled the tub with too much bubble bath, sitting in the mountain of suds and listening to the sounds of their voices crashing into each other behind the closed door of the den. I waited for one of them to emerge, letting my skin prune as the water turned from nearly scalding to barely lukewarm. Once the bubbles had all disappeared, I gave up, but as I wrapped myself in towels, I heard the den door open and the sound of bodies shuffling around downstairs. Their voices were silent now. I moved into my bedroom, running a comb through my wet tangles with little impact until someone appeared in my doorway.

It was my father.

"How long have you known?" he asked. I heard the front door slam and the family car start up in the driveway. I imagined for a moment that Betsi had convinced my mother to drive her to Graceland, and I toyed with the idea of sprinting from the room to join them.

"A while." I wasn't sure if he was mad or just wanted a timeline. He sat down next to me on the bed. I couldn't look him in the face or control the tears spilling out of my eyes.

"It's my fault, isn't it?" I choked on my words but managed to cough up a few more. "I should've said something sooner."

My father grabbed both of my arms and pulled me close, hugging me harder than he had in my entire life. "This. Is. Not. Your. Fault." He made each word its own statement. "None of it. No one is angry at you." I stayed buried in the cave of his shoulder for a while, his hand anchored on the back of my head, holding my wet hair.

"Does anyone else know?" he finally asked, interrupting our moment of silence.

"I don't think so," I lied, thinking about Jack.

"I'm not sure what we're going to say—to Uncle Tim or anyone else—or if we'll say anything at all. Sometimes there's a good reason for keeping secrets. I hope you can understand."

Yes, I can, I thought, deciding right then that I would never tell anyone about Barry's note—not my parents or Uncle Tim, certainly not Betsi. Not even Jack. No one.

* * * * *

Later that night, Peter, our mother, and I gather around the dinner table for pizza from Giacomo's. My father's chair remains empty, but at least Mom has stopped filling in the spaces with her chatter about sixteen-hour sales and sightings of neighbors at the grocery store.

"Going to Hannah's again tonight?" Mom asks, passing me the Greek salad that had been dumped from the take-out container into a glass bowl to make it look better.

"Not tonight," I tell her, giving myself a generous second helping.

"Oh, are you babysitting? I keep getting my weekends mixed up."

"How come guys never babysit?" Peter asks out of nowhere. "I don't remember us ever having a guy babysitter."

"That's because we never did," I say, throwing my napkin at him. "No, I'm not babysitting tonight. I thought maybe I'd just stay home and we could watch a movie or something."

My mother sets her fork down on her plate and forgets her usual manners, asking with a full mouth, "You mean with me?"

"If that's okay."

She tries to swallow quickly so she can speak before I change my mind. "That's a great idea. We can go to the video store after we're done. Is there something in particular you want to see?" She wants so much to please and set things right.

I try to make it easier for her. "Why don't we see what's on TV? I bet there's some old Joan Crawford movie, or Katharine Hepburn." She sits quietly. "You like both of them, right?" I check.

"Right," she says. Her eyes begin to well—just slightly.

"Mom."

"Right!" she says, shifting her tone. "I think that sounds perfect."

* * * * *

Peter falls asleep before the opening credits of *Whatever Happened to Baby Jane?* finish rolling, and our mother isn't too far behind him. We've all seen the movie before, but I stay glued until the scene when Bette Davis serves Joan Crawford the dead bird—even the sight of the covered tray can give me nightmares. I slide the remote out of Peter's hand and turn off the TV, slipping an afghan over each of them and leaving before the bird scene comes on.

I shut my bedroom door gently behind me, wandering over to my bookshelf and flipping through the stack of Betsi's records. Mom gave me temporary custody of the music and player, saying it was too fragile to try and ship to Betsi right now. I run my hands over the worn covers, studying the evolution of Elvis in the photographs. There are other records too, and tonight I choose one of my favorites, eyeballing the grooves in the record to find the song I want. I set the needle down in the right place on the first try, and the music quietly fills the room as I remember Barry twirling me around his kitchen.

I walk over to my closet, kneeling down and reaching through the hanging clothes until my hands find the small duffel bag. I pull it out carefully so I don't disrupt anything around it, placing it in my lap and unzipping it to make sure the jacket is still tucked inside. I look back over my shoulder, but even with the music playing, there are signs of stirring coming from downstairs.

"Just once more," I tell myself again. The jacket still has traces of Barry, his woodsy scent, and I am afraid of wearing it all away. But I slip my arms into it anyway, swimming in the largeness and wrapping the excess around my body like a blanket. The pockets are completely empty now—I hid all of those things away so no one would ever find them—but the varsity pins are still attached. I crawl under my sheets, listening to Elton John and falling asleep into Barry. Tonight for the first time, it's not anger that takes me there.

* * * * *

Sunday morning I come downstairs just before 10 A.M. and the house seems quiet, as if it's still asleep. I wander into the kitchen and open the refrigerator, then drink large gulps of juice directly from the container.

"You know that makes your mother crazy."

My father's voice shocks me, causing the juice to dribble down my chin. I turn around and find him seated at the breakfast table, drinking coffee and reading the Business section of the paper.

"Jesus, Dad! You freaked me out. I didn't know you were here," I snap, wiping my chin.

"Sorry," he says, smirking.

"Are you *laughing* at me?"

"You are so busted." The words sound completely out of place coming from his mouth, and I can't help but giggle.

"Yeah, well . . ." I sit down across from him, admitting defeat. "Maybe we can keep this just between us?"

"You've got a deal," he says, passing me the *Parade* magazine. "Let's call a do-over and try this again. Good morning, Presley."

"What did you just say?" I ask.

"Good morning?"

"No. Before that."

"Oh. A do-over. You know what that is, don't you?" he asks, sipping his coffee.

"Yes," I tell him. "I know exactly what it is."

I stand up and pour myself a mug, waiting for him to object, but he simply mentions, "There's creamer on the table."

"Where did everyone go?"

"Your mother got an overwhelming desire to make chocolate-chip pancakes, but of course we didn't have all of the ingredients. Peter insisted on going with her to make sure she got the right ones—"

"Bittersweet dark," I say, finishing his sentence. "What's the occasion?" Chocolate-chip pancakes are usually reserved for birthday breakfasts.

"I think the occasion is that there *is* no occasion."

I nod as if I understand, flipping through the pages of *Parade* and listening to my father shake his section of the paper into place. From the view out the kitchen window, it looks like it might storm soon, and I wonder whether it will pass over us without breaking or if the temperatures will drop with the rain. I want to ask my father when he got here and how long he's staying, but instead I pretend to concentrate on a crossword puzzle, ignoring the definitions and clues provided and filling in each space with whatever letters come to mind.

* * * * *

My father stays for two rounds of pancakes, a light lunch of crackers and cheese and grapes, and even dinner, breaking out the charcoals and grilling bratwurst and corn on the cob. The rain holds off, and we are all still pretending it's later in the year than it really is, drinking fresh iced tea from the plastic tumblers we use for picnics at the Pier Park. After the table is cleared and the dishes are tucked into the washer, I ask to be excused, mumbling something about English homework before I escape to my room.

I sit at my desk, placing my textbooks underneath the glow of the table lamp. Forty-five minutes pass as I stare at the faint blue lines on the piece of paper, trying to remember the order of words.

Dear Betsi. I write it for the seventh time in cursive, but it looks too formal and elegant. I decide to switch back to block printing, crumpling the piece of paper into a ball and tossing it toward my wastebasket. I expect it to fall onto the carpet with my other misfires, but I make the shot, earning two points. It's a start.

I pull out a fresh, clean piece and begin again.

About the Author

Sarah Grace McCandless is a Midwest native and a graduate of Michigan State University. She is the author of *Grosse Pointe Girl: Tales from a Suburban Adolescence.* After spending eight years in Portland, Oregon, she currently lives in Washington, D.C., and writes for several publications, including *Daily Candy, Venus,* and *Mudsugar.*

Also available by
Sarah Grace McCandless

In Grosse Pointe, Michigan, the new girl in town discovers that social rank is determined by the age of your money and the dryness of your martini.

"Sarah Grace McCandless writes with humor and compassion and honesty about the most embarrassing time in all our lives, those terrible years between the first crush and the first orgasm. No matter which side of the tracks you come from, *Grosse Pointe Girl* will hit you where you live."
—Pam Houston, author of *Cowboys Are My Weakness*